GHETTO FANATASY

A 8-5-0 SERIES

(10 minutes til 9)

"THE BEGINNING"

GHETTO FANTASY

Have you ever had a dream, a fantasy, or a standard of living, that you vision yourself obtaining someday? Shit, let's be honest. We all do!!

Face- to- face with the circumstances, that enslave our thoughts constantly, I grew up with that same fantasy. I had a want, a desire, a need, for the things that seem to carry that stare of admiration, in other's eyes...

Yeah... that look right there!!

The cars, the clothes, the jewels, the hoes, and...Oh, let's not forget the dope. You know that shit that gets a junky high? That kills, steals, and destroys a mother's child...But most importantly, it employed the poor?... with GREED... and a STRONG desire to succeed.

Now, if only the proper instructions were applied! I probably wouldn't be on this side... Doing this bid, away from kids.

I want you to take a journey with me, and I guarantee, you may find yourself along the way. We call it the game, but every character has a different script. Look at my mistakes and analyze my flaws, in which I am not ashamed to admit... Because the more I hear y'all speak... the more I realize... "A lot of y'all!"...WERE EVEN DUMBER THAN ME!"

Have you ever had a dream? A fantasy? Now, what if that fantasy suddenly became reality. Could you handle it? Could you subdue the pressure of having to constantly watch your back? Not knowing who to trust? Because trust can be a weak man's downfall! And Love?... What's that?... Is that an emotion expressed between family and friends, or a woman and man? I think not, because to love me, you had to hate yourself totally. Cause See... I wanted it all..." Point Blank!" So, take a minute or two to think.

Could you truly love me without wanting a piece of what you see? Hell NO! Therefore I define "Love" as a Benefit!". An enemy's strategy, for something they want and desperate to get.

And That's How This Story Begins!!

CHAPTER 1

Series 1 “THE BEGINNING”

1990 Morris Court Projects aka “THE HILL"

Knocking (Bam, Bam).... (Bam, Bam, Bam)

"Boy, get your behind up, before you be late foe that school bus. You got twenty minutes before that school bus be pulling up out there!"

(Bam, Bam, Bam)...

”Bleak, Get up and get ready!!"

"Yes, Ma’am!” Bleak yelled out.

” DAM “he whispered to himself as he climbed out of bed, and drifted into the bathroom. With sleep still clogged in his mind, he stood in a daze as he stared in the mirror at the image before him.

Brad Lamar Staples “Bleak,” was what everyone called him. That was the nickname his father gave him when he was born. Who’s now serving 2 life sentences in federal prison for the shooting death of an undercover narcotics officer, whom he was attempting to rob.

The officers thought they were going to purchase two and a half kilos of cocaine. But instead, one officer was wounded, and another killed. He ran for several months, but someone eventually snitched his whereabouts, and he was apprehended somewhere in Texas.

Bleak, now thirteen years old, could only vaguely remember anything about his pops. Considering that fact that he was only two years old when that incident occurred. Now with his pops being absent all these years, he really didn’t care to remember. But the streets always carried respect for OG’s, so he always heard stories about his pops.

"Boy! Why the hell you standing there looking stupid? "..."Wash your face, brush your teeth, and take your ass out there to that bus stop!"..."I made you a sausage egg and cheese sandwich to take with... on your way out the door!!"

"Yes Ma'am!"

Bleak immediately washed up, got dressed, and headed out the door. He kissed his mother on the cheek while saying, "I'll see you later," as he raced down the sidewalk to the bus stop.

His mother's name was Luceal Perkins but everyone called her "Lu Lu," for short. Lu Lu was smart and beautiful. She wore her hair short and stylish. She stood about 5'6, with a honey brown complexion, and every one of the male gender viewed her as being sexy as hell. Lu Lu had a nice petite shape, perfect size round butt, and a set of breasts that stayed in position even without the support of a bra, and they bounced with every step that she made.

Lu Lu's only mistake in her mind, was that she made bad choices when it came to men. She conceived Bleak at the age of eighteen, while attempting to attend a community college seeking to build a career in becoming a RN. But that idea managed to fade away when she discovered she was two and a half months pregnant. So, she then moved from under her mother's roof, after applying for public housing. For her and Beankie could stay together, and raise their unborn child. The projects was never their destination. But it was, their only alternative at the time.

Lu Lu planned on returning to school a year after Bleak was born, but Beankie talked her out of it. He promised that he would always take care of them. The money was good at time, but mainly he just wanted them under his security and protection, at all times. He sort of felt incomplete with either of them outside his presence.

Benjamin Aton Staples, aka, Beankie

Beankie was an all-around hustler, that's all he knew. He sold drugs (crack, cocaine), He robbed people (locals, out-of-towners, it didn't matter). He burglarized jewelry stores and houses, and even stole cars from time to time, which he would sell to a chop shop in Texas. However, in whatever profession a dollar could be obtained? Beankie was a part of it, a true "All-Around Hustler!"

Most people found him difficult to understand, but very few questioned his motives. They just viewed Beankie as being a young, greedy, wild ass individual, whom only Lu Lu had the power to control. But deep down, underneath his menacing ways, Beankie had a good side. He just found enjoyment in terrorizing the proud, those who assumed they had heart and couldn't be touched or tested. But through Beankie's eyes, they were weak, they hid behind money which compelled them to believe they had heart. They talked it, but when it came to walking it? That heart went in the opposite direction. In Beankie's mind, "Shit, FEAR, was more precious than Gold, because it's a weakness... that keeps on giving."

Beankie didn't smoke, drink, or use drugs, and nor did he engage in any sexual activities with other women. He was solely dedicated to Lu Lu.

He invested his money in various things. Clothes, jewelry, hand guns, and two his and her's '76 Chevy Caprice classics, as well as anything else to keep Lu Lu happy.

As for the Chevy's, no one really saw how Beankie's looked, because he immediately placed his in storage the day he bought it. He then purchased a small minivan that he used to get around in.

Now as for Lu Lu's Chevy, the whole city saw it, you couldn't help but to see it. Beankie put it in the game. It was champagne pink, with a maroon rag top, and it sat on a set of 30 spoke cragar rims and vogues tires (trues and Vogues). The inside had plush maroon seats with silver leather trim. But the dark limo tinted windows, that hid Lu Lu so perfectly, was what really gave it that " Gangsta Appeal". Along with the chrome grill and the tag underneath it that read, "DON'T STARE," in dark maroon wicked letters, as if it were written in blood. A few people would ask Beankie what it meant, and with an evil smirk he would simply reply

"Just Don't Violate, and find out!!"

****

"There go bleak, right there!"..." Wsup homie?"..." We thought you was playing hooky today, but Lu Lu made your ass get out that bed huh?" D-Boy yelled, while laughing at the same time.

D-Boy (Daryl Wiggins), Crash (Edwin Dees), and Tig (Terrance Dukes), were Bleaks' homeboys. "The Baby Hill Boys," was what the old heads called them, because they were four little bad ass individuals, who were always up to no good. Fighting, stealing bikes, and all other sorts of juvenile related activities. But as for Bleak and Tig, they always managed to keep a low profile because neither of their mothers played or slacked up on disciplining them. So for Bleak and Tig, an ass whooping was something they sought to avoid as much as possible.

D-Boy on the other hand, didn't give a damn. His pops he never knew, and his mother, Sue Ann, smoked crack. D-Boy loved her, but he just didn't respect her, because basically she didn't respect herself. Sue Ann would often prance around the projects in tiny sleazy clothes that would expose the majority of her body parts. Or, at times, she would just have on a long t-shirt with nothing on underneath. It embarrassed D-Boy at times because he knew what she was, in-fact everyone knew.

Sue Ann was a "Trick". She traded her body for a high that controlled her mind. Sue Ann and D-Boy stayed with her mother, which was D-Boy's grandmother, who lost both of her legs due to diabetes. But she was as sweet as could be, and loved her grandson regardless of what he did.

Ms. Anna Bell was her name; she was like the down ass grandmother that everyone loved. When the police would come around, to do a sting, are just to harass people. Here came Ms. Anna Bell rolling down the side walk in her wheel chair cussing up a storm.

"Why ya'll always come around here fucking with honest folks?"..." Go fuck with your own kind!... Y'all don't have anything else better to do?"..." I tell yah, if I had both of my legs, I'd stand up and slap the shit outta one you pink face muthafuckas"... "1-by-1! ...Go harass your own!"

The funny thing about it, the police even respected her, too. Ms. Anna Bell loved talking to Bleak, mainly about his pops and how much she saw the same traits in him.

Now, as for Crash, his whole family sold drugs. Mom, pops, uncles, aunties, and cousins. Everybody. It was a family trade, which he would inherit eventually.

****

"Bleak! Tig hit a lick last night!"

D-Boy yelled, with a smirk on his face.

"Yeah man, I went to go take out the trash for Ma'Dukes, and a wood pulled up trying to cop a 100 piece. I ran in the house, grabbed an old bar of soap; cut it up, and "BAM Nigga!" A hundred dollar bill!"

Tig quickly pulled the bill out of his pocket and continued.

"Man, I was telling D-Boy and Crash"..."Fuck stealing bikes!" Dog, I'm finta start selling soap!"

Everyone begin laughing, while at the same time that the school bus was pulling up.

They all climbed on the bus along with two other boys, and five girls. Kiesha, Kim, Janay, Tasha, and Candice aka Caddy. The two boys were Jake and Dave, who no one liked. Everyone called them the project nerds, and whose mothers considered them better than the rest of the kids in the projects.

Meanwhile, Lu Lu was peeping out her bedroom window, as she watched Bleak and the other kids board the school bus. After the bus pulled off, she went back in the kitchen, sat down, and finished eating breakfast. Afterwards, she washed up the few dishes, and got ready for work as usual.

Lu Lu worked as a cashier at Joe's Seafood and besides smelling fish all day and dealing with all sorts of different attitudes. It was an okay job.

She reported to work after Bleak went to school and would be off before he made it home. Plus, she was off on weekends and most holidays. The little money that she made, met most of her needs. Because all she had to do, was keep the Chevy up and running that Beankie bought her over thirteen years ago.

Lu Lu also received $500 a month from Beankie's uncle, a man named Sammy, whom she knew of but never met. When Beankie was sentenced to life plus life, he told Lu Lu that Sammy would be in touch. She and Beankie had gone through seventy-two grand that they had stashed, on a lawyer who really couldn't help him at all.

Since then, Lu Lu always received a money order in the mail at the end of every month, that begun over eleven years ago, and still continued 'til this day.

Lu Lu always wanted to thank Sammy personally, but never knew how to get in touch with him. Because the envelopes that the money orders came in never presented a return address. So after a few years, she eventually figured that he didn't want to be thanked, so she thanked "GOD" in return.

Now, on this particular morning as she drove to work, she noticed a familiar face at a gas station while she was paused at the red light. The face was that of Carlos Jackson. Formerly a pretty boy, now a dingy, weightless, junky, she had dated a little over a year ago. That was until he stole six diamond rings and four bracelets, filled with stones of various colors, and tried to trade them off for cocaine, to a guy in the same projects in which she lived. A guy that knew her and respected Beankie.

Now of course Carlos received the beat down that he deserved. But afterwards, Lu Lu felt embarrassed, because everyone knew Carlos was shooting cocaine. Everyone except for her!

The guy that officially kicked Carlos's ass, and returned Lu Lu her belongings, stood in Lu Lu's door way and looked her eye-to-eye,

"Hey, Ms. Lu Lu, Baby, I know Beankie doing life... And as a G, he more than likely suggested for you not to prolong yours"... "But you're a product of royalty, so with all due respect... "Baby, Stick to the Code!" You can't replace gold with silver and expect it to maintain the same value"...." Anyway Ms. Lu Lu"... You have blessed day. .."And Please!"... "MAINTAIN YOUR VALUE!"

After he walked away, Lu Lu stood in the door way puzzled. She didn't quite know what he meant, but in a strange sense she figured he was right.

As the light changed, she drove and began to think about all the men she had dated in her life, which were only four. She thought about them in order from last to first:

Carlos- The pretty boy now a dingy, weightless, junky.

Teddy- The service man, who thought he could stop by and hit every time he came in town.

Rico- The wanna-be player.

And Beankie- The gangster that fucked up her life.

Which she knew wasn't true. She loved Beankie, he was her first, and she cherished every moment they shared together. The only problem in her mind was that he didn't love himself, because if you love yourself, you wouldn't place yourself in situations that could and eventually would make your existence obsolete.

But all and all, she still loved Beankie with her soul, and made a vow to herself that she would never truly love another man, nor attempt to establish a real relationship, especially after the shit Carlos pulled. From here on out, she would just have a friend for sexual satisfaction. Nothing more, nothing less, and not all the time, so she resumed her relationship with Teddy, the service man!

****

Now in school, Bleak, D-Boy, Crash, and Tig, were ninth grade celebrities. They were always fresh, and each carried their own unique style.

Crash wore Polo everything from head to toe. A lot of girls in school just started calling him Polo, instead of Crash, and he loved it.

D-Boy was always dressed in a fresh white T shirt with heavy starched Levi jeans. His main thing was his sneakers, and if anyone accidently stepped on or brushed against them. You would have a ring side seat to a title bout.

D-Boy loved to fight and he was good at it. And most of the time his shoes were the cause.

Bleak was versatile, but he mainly liked velour sweat suits by the brands Fila, Adidas, Nike, and Christian Dior.

As for Tig, he dressed normal. He was always clean. He just didn't wear anything that stood out or turned heads. But that's how Tig was, he didn't like attention.

The group liked school for various reasons. But D-Boy on the other hand, mainly came to fight and protect his homeboys, as he often jokingly expressed at times. The only class he would attempt to show interest in was math, and that was only because he and Bleak shared the same math class.

He knew Bleak was serious about learning and graduating when the time came. Because he made a vow to Lu Lu that he would.

In a sense, they all revolved around Bleak, and he knew it. Deep down in his heart, Bleak always felt that he would be someone of importance. He didn't know who, but that emotion kept growing.

1992- 2 years later.

Crash and D-Boy were seated at Bugaboos' kitchen table cutting up 6 cookie shaped ounces of crack cocaine. D-Boy asked Crash,

“Damn man, why you cuttin' them 20's so damn big?"

"Cause Boy, the bigger they are, the faster they gone fall in a fiend hand. Shit, ain't no need to try to make a mill, off free shit."

Crash replied, with a silly smile on his face.

D-Boy began examining the pieces he had cut up himself, and whispered to himself, “Damn! Well, these gone be dimes!”

Buggaloo entered the kitchen after over-hearing what D-Boy asked Crash. As he approached looking over Crash's shoulder he exclaimed,

"Damn Crash, You Right! A Nigga can't pass them up!”

Buggaloo then looked at the pile of pieces in front of D-Boy, and asked in a slow funny proper English tone.

"Now Sir, May I inquire, WHAT ARE THOSE??"

Crash immediately started laughing, and Buggaloo followed.

D-Boy stared at them both.

“I don't know why y'all laughing. Nigga these Big Boy Dimes ...Right Here!”

“I presume that you're absolutely correct Sir, they better be,” Buggaloo responded as he continued laughing.

==

Buggaloo was an ex-Vietnam veteran, now crack head who, was funny as hell. They loved being around Buggaloo, even when they were younger because he always kept them laughing. That's how he got the name Buggaloo, because people would contribute to his habit just to him talking about folks. And some just did it in hope, that they wouldn't be a part of the joke.

Buggaloo once had a girlfriend, whose name was Shaneal, but he had talked about her so much, that she eventually ended up leaving. D-Boy would often joke with him saying.

"You See?.., That's the same reason Shaneal left your ass. You talk to damn much; ...you need to practice shutting up SOME DAM TIME!"

Buggaloo always had a comeback, something silly with a rhyme involved.

"Left ME? Silly Rabbit, you need to learn something, before you try to turn something. My house, My rules!".." A bitch have to pay dues!:.."Now, when and if those dues... become past dues!"..."Then Baby, Buggaloo got some BAD NEWS!"..."Hoe!"... "YOU GOT, TO GO!"..."So Boy, like I said ...you better learn something...before you try to turn something!"..."I kicked her ass out!"... But SHIT!"..."The Buggaloo still kind-of MISS her though!"

Buggaloo was silly as hell, and his apartment became the spot where they cut up their drugs and sold them off his back porch, with his help of course.

The back porch was close to Buggaloos bedroom window, and when a customer came up, they would simply hand the money to Crash or D-Boy. Then, Buggaloo dropped the crack in the customers hand through a hole in the screen of the bedroom window.

They often reflected on the events that lead them into the game. This occurred about three and a half months ago. A guy from the other side of town, whose name was Stats, came through the projects in his Cadillac bumping the "Freaky Tales," by Too Short.

D-Boy and Crash were chasing Tig, because he snatched the blunt they were smoking on that early Saturday morning. They usually always played around in that fashion.

As Bleak was coming outside, Tig ran right by him yelling, "Look homie, them niggas slow, look at 'em!"

Crash and D-Boy yelled back, "Grab 'em, Bleak, grab 'em!"

Bleak stood there laughing as he shouted back, "Shit! He too fast!"

As Stats was riding through, Tig ran right in front of his car, which forced him to slam on his brakes. Tig stopped,

"My Bad Man, I'm sorry!" as he was trying to catch his breath.

Stats turned his music down.

"Yo Bad? You Sorry? Lil Nigga, You almost got hit, and you can bet your ASS!... I would've kept pushing!"

D-Boy and Crash were walking up at the time, with Bleak only a few steps behind.

Stats looked over after seeing Bleak,

"Bleak, Wsup Boy. That's one of your Lil Homies?"

"Yeah," Bleak confirmed with a serious look on his face.

Stats smirked.

"O Ok, That's Wsup. Well, you need to keep his lil ass in line cuz he almost got hit!!"

He turned his music back up and hit the horn as he slowly pulled off.

They all stood in the middle of the street and watched him as he drove on, then stopped and parked in front of Ms. Anna Bell's apartment. He then got out and proceeded to walk to the front door.

Tig broke the silence.

"Man, I don't like that NIGGA!"

Mainly because he felt the tension everyone else was harboring.

"Us either," Bleak replied, as if he spoke for D-Boy and Crash.

D-Boy confirmed (in a semi sad tone) "Yeah, and he going in there to halla at Sue Ann!"

Which they all knew, and the idea made them even madder.

Bleak, as if he suddenly snapped.

"Man, Fuck That!"..." We finta get this nigga!"

Everyone shook their heads in agreement

"Let's do it!"

They all headed towards Ms. Anna Bell's apartment. D-Boy ran in to check and see was the coast clear.

After a few seconds D-Boy returned.

"Everything straight"… "Grandma Sleep!"…" And he in the room, with Sue Ann."

Bleak immediately walked towards Stats Cadillac and checked the doors, but they were locked.

Tig and Crash were looking through the car's windows but didn't see anything of value.

D-Boy whispered.

"Man, Watch out!" as he retrieved an empty beer bottle from the ground and threw it through the driver's side window.

Bleak then stuck his hand inside to push the button to unlock the doors.

Tig quickly climbed in the passenger's side, and opened the glove compartment to search, while at the same time pushing the button to unlock the trunk.

They all proceeded to search the car. Looking under the seats, pulling on the door panels, trying to see if there were hidden compartments, but everyone stopped when Crash yelled from the trunk

"Yo, I Think I Found Something!"

Bleak and Tig quickly hopped out as they all took off running with Crash's discovery.

Stats ran out of the apartment, with his shirt off and pants half way down, shortly after he heard the sound of glass breaking and had peeped out the window and saw that it was his car.

As he got to the car, he saw Bleak and the rest of the group running away.

"O Hell Naw, Y'all Lil Niggas done fucked up, I swear… I'ma KILL ONE of you lil Muthafuckers!"

Then as he noticed that his trunk was open, he became furious and louder

"Oh Yeah, Boy!"…"I SWEAR! Ya'll GONE DIE, about this!" … "I swear to God, boy… on my Mama!"…"Y'all GONE HAVE TO ANSWER GOD!"

After a while, people started to come outside towards the commotion questioning.

“YO STATS”...” Wsup Man?"..”What’s Happening???”

The boys, were long gone by then.

Stats just stood by his car pissed.

"I’m good...but boy I promise you”...”All them Lil Niggas GONE DIE!”...” I Promise YOU, THAT!”

After a while of hearing Stats, continuous repeated threats, someone in the crowd yelled out,

“Hold up homeboy”...”Let’s get this shit straight right now...cuz you ain’t killing shit out here!”... As a matter of fact”... Nigga Roll Out!”...”Before shit get PHYSICAL!”...”Cuz you ain’t killing shit out here, especially no kids!”

Stats noticed people were starting to get riled up, after that speech he was giving. He quickly came to the realization that his best option at that time, was to leave.

Stats hopped in his car, hit the ignition, and then attempted to back out of the parking lot, while hitting his horn for people to move, as they stood all around his car.

Suddenly someone in the crowd shouted out.

“Man, Fuck ThAT!”...”BEAT THAT NIGGA .ASS!”...”Don’t let him leave up out here!”

And that’s when all hell broke loose.

Someone opened the car door, and attempted to pull him out. While others, began kicking, stomping, and throwing objects at and into his vehicle.

Stats immediately hit the gas pedal while throwing the Cadillac in reverse, but someone quickly hit the gear shift into park.

After a brief but tense struggle, they eventually drug him out, and it was all over.

By the time the police and paramedics arrived, it was too late. Stats, wasn't dead, but he looked pretty close to it.

The paramedics hoped out and quickly placed him on a stretcher, then took off. While a few police officers stuck around trying to obtain information, as they waited for the Cadillac to be towed, or what was left of it.

Bleak, Tig, Crash, and D-Boy, ran to Buggaloo's apartment with the bag Crash grabbed out of the trunk of Stats Cadillac.

As they dumped the contents of the bag on Buggaloo's kitchen table, they realized they had hit a good lick, a lick that will surely inject consequences and repercussions: 6 1/2cookies of crack cocaine, 3 pounds of weed, a 357 hand gun, and a little over two grand in cash.

Crash yelled out excitedly,

"Shit, I know we gon' spilt everything...but this backpack...This one right here! MINE!"

Everyone looked crazy for a second, until realizing the polo logo imprint on the bag pack.

Bleak, sent Buggaloo to the store to grab some Swisher blunts, while they sat at the table to split the money, which came to a total of $560 a piece.

When Buggaloo returned with the Cigar blunts. They each rolled up 2 a piece, then everyone lit up.

Buggaloo stood up (Clowning around as usual)

"Hold on Ladies and Gentlemen... and excuse me for the Lady part!"..."But Anyways.. Let us all tap blunts together as a toast... Cuz BOY!... Y'all lil asses on NOW!... Shit y'all got dope, money, weed, and a big ass pistol'... But all y'all missing.... is ONE THANG!"

D-Boy asked (as a thin cloud of smoke followed his words)

"Oh Yeah, Fool?.... And what's that?

"That?"..,"Sir, will be a razor blade... cuz the Loo-ster got to get paid... Now chop chop, and make me happy."

As the laughter came to an end, Bleak grabbed the half of a cookie, of crack and slid it across the table in Buggaloo's direction.

"Sir...We don't need a razor blade!... You Do!"..." Unless you gone' smoke it all at once!"

D-Boy quickly cut in

"Shit, and if he DO!"..."His ass better fall out!"..."Cuz I'ma stick that broom in i

em !"... "An bring 'em back to life!"

"Whatever!...Lil Boy." Buggaloo replied as he looked back at Bleak.

"See that's why I like you. That's some real Playa shit!"..." and D-Boy... that lady I was respectfully acknowledging in this piece ..."Was You!"...YOU, Lil Bitch!"

(D-Boy and Buggaloo always went at it the most, but it was all love).

As Buggaloo grabbed the cookie, he yelled out,

"Shaneal!"..."Baby, bring your ass in here!"

Shaneal came out of the bedroom mad,

"Damn, Buggaloo what the hell you want? ....You know I was watching my stories...I know 1 dam thang ...Nigga, this shit better be important."

Buggaloo smirked.

"BABY!"... "Shut the Hell UP!"... "AND LOOK!"

When Shaneal noticed all the drugs on table and the cookie Buggaloo was holding, she began smiling.

"Baby... Thanks to My Friends, we gon get high, and get paid"... and afterwards, baby... I'ma take you to get your month fix!"... "Buy you some outfits!" ..."and then ...LET you see the WORLD."

Shaneal blushed.

"Aww Baby!"..."Dam... I'm excited," ... "Where we going?"

Buggaloo chuckled.

"We?"..." Baby, I said you!"... "I'm staying here with my Young-ins!" ..." See we are about to Blow UP!"... "And we don't need any ugly Folks, on the team.

Buggaloo was silly as hell and he always kept them laughing. They loved and respected him and the feeling was mutual. Buggaloo loved and respected them too.

They remained ducked off in his apartment until night fell, while trying to figure out their next move to get rid of the drugs they stole.

After an hr of silence, Bleak stood up.

"Ok, here's the plan; we sit on this silently for a month, or two, just to see how everything play out"... "At the same time, we gon study the study this game from every angle...Police and all!"..." Meanwhile, me and Tig gone start selling some of the weed at school!" "Now, D-Boy, you don't like school and Ms. Anna Bell don't really sweat you bout going." "Crash, your people the same, but we do need you to see how they cut they stuff up, so we can have ours just a lil bit bigger"... "That's only if that's alright with you!"

Crash laughed.

"Man, my people wholesale, so all we got to do is stick to the small shit. If we decide to continue, we can cop from my Auntie Dow. She stays in New Orleans, but she comes in town every month to drop shit off on my folks. She down as hell, and it wouldn't be problem to slide in on the action!"

Bleak was happy. "Cool!"

They all slapped hands and went home, leaving everything with Buggaloo. As D-Boy was leaving, he looked back at Buggaloo,

"Man, don't make us kill you!"

Buggaloo laughed.

"Ok Lil Boy!"..."But in the Meantime in- between time!"..." Let them Big Ass Feet"..."Work on killing that Concrete!"..."GET THE HELL MY House!"

Despite Buggaloo's habits and jokes, they all loved and trusted him, and he knew it.

What led up to Buggaloo's apartment becoming their official spot was, on one Sunday morning, D-Boy was posted in the alley, which was a gap between apartment buildings. He was trying to catch crack sales before they made it across the street, to the neighborhood store, where everyone stood and conducted business. After a while, D-Boy's impatience over-powered his judgment, so he said to himself "fuck it," as he made his way across the street to the store where everyone else was.

Ten minutes after he crossed and posted up, unmarked police cars pulled up quickly and jumped out. Someone yelled, "5-0! White folks in your face," but it was too late. Officers grabbed D-Boy, and everyone else in front of the store, and made them stand and face the wall, with their hands behind their heads. They proceeded to search everyone one by one. After the officer searched D-Boy and didn't find anything, they sent him back across the street.

Crash was standing in the alley laughing as D-Boy approached.

"Dog, what made you take your dumb ass over there? You know that shit hot!"

As D-Boy got closer, Crashed whispered,

"You good? What you do with the shit?"

D-Boy had his hand on his chest.

"Man, I swallowed it and my chest beating fast as hell!"

"You Okay? You Alright?" ..."Man...Say Something!"

D-Boy walked right passed him, with his hand over his chest, heading towards his apartment.

Crash ran to Bleak's apartment and knocked on his bedroom window. As the blinds moved, Crash saw Bleak's sleepy eyes looking at him, so he fanned his hand in the "hurry up, come here," motion.

After a few minutes or so, Bleak came out.

Crash immediately filled him on what had happened as they were jogging to catch up with D-Boy, as he was entering his front door. They entered as well right behind him.

Ms. Anna Bell was seated in her wheelchair in the living room watching T.V. She looked at D-Boy,

"Daryl, Boy what's wrong with you? You ok?"

"Naw Grandma...My stomach feels funny and my chest beating fast."

Ms. Anna Bell looked into D-Boys eyes, as Bleak and Crash stood by watching. Then she turned towards Bleak.

"Baby, go in the fridge and grab that carton of milk!"

Bleak immediately did what she requested and returned, handing the carton of milk to Ms. Anna Bell. Ms. Anna Bell opened the milk and handed it to D-Boy, while telling him to drink as much as he can. She then instructed him go into the bathroom and stick his finger down his throat until he starts to throw up.

Bleak and Crash followed behind him and stood in the doorway of the bathroom.

"Uggh, Uggh, Ugggh,",

Were the sounds he made as he continued to throw up.

After a few minutes, Ms. Anna Bell rolled into the bathroom. Bleak and Crash moved out her way, as she tossed D-Boy a towel so he could wash his face and hands. Then, before she backed her wheelchair out of the bathroom's doorway, Ms. Anna Bell said, while shaking her head in disbelief,

"Daryl"....Baby, crack is to be sold or smoked... Now, if you want to start something new by eating it, you go right ahead. BUT I guarantee you will beat me and your mama to the grave."

Bleak and Crash stood looking stupid and shocked. D-Boy grumbled, "What y'all looking all dumb foe?...Boy, my Grandma aint stupid, she know everything!"

From that point on, they made Buggaloo's apartment their spot, and figured out a way to never have drugs in their possession. And that was simply by: getting the money first, and having Buggaloo drop the product in the customer's hand through a hole in the screen of his bedroom window. The lesser risk would provide a lesser chance, of getting caught up.

****

(Back at Buggaloo's Apartment)

After the drugs were cut up, Crash and D-Boy's count added up to $7,300. Bleak and Tig had already begun selling some of the weed at school, they bagged up $4,000 in dimes. The total count after all the drugs were sold, would be $11,360.

CHAPTER 2

(2 Months Later)

All the drugs were sold, they had a count of $10,550, which was $810 off from what was expected. However, everyone was more than happy with what they had, considering that they were only fourteen years old. D-Boy was the oldest at fifteen, and they were all looking at ten grand from having nothing It made a young man's ego untouchable. The game became a part of life at that point.

Bleak and Tig still continued to go to school, and kept selling weed to their classmates. Especially the white kids, whose families supplied them with healthy allowances.

Bleak and Crash also negotiated a deal with Crash's Auntie Dow. Every two weeks when she came in town, they would purchase five pounds of weed at $700 a pound (which Dow only paid $500 for), and they purchased a quarter of a kilo of cooked crack for $5,000 (which was only seven ounces of cocaine, cooked up to weigh 252 grams). Dow figured the boys didn't know the difference, and she was right, because they kept buying more from her every time she came, and they profited off of every package. This kept everyone happy, especially Dow.

****

Lu Lu kind of figured that Bleak had gotten involved with selling drugs, but she never questioned him because he continued to go to school. Plus, she hadn't been feeling well, and a lie would only upset her more.

Lu Lu had begun staying in her bed all day, for days at a time. It had gotten to the point that she quit her job at Joe's seafood and just laid around the house. Bleak would continuously ask, "Mama, you okay?"

"Yeah, baby, I'm good," Lu Lu paused, "Mama just hasn't been feeling herself lately!"

Lu Lu also had lost a little weight, and her appetite wasn't the same. Bleak was concerned, but not especially worried. He just figured she needed a break from both working, and the stress of being a single mom. To Bleak, they were both taking a toll on her.

Two years later

Lu Lu was now thirty-six years old, and Bleak was seventeen, completing his last year of school. The day of graduation, Lu Lu was there, along with Tig's mother, D-Boy, and Crash.

Bleak and Tig felt good walking across the stage, as they were handed their diplomas, while family and friends cheered them on.

Lu Lu couldn't help but to start crying. Bleak immediately ran to where she stood and embraced her with huge and smile, while saying, "Mama, I told you! You happy now? I love you!"

Lu Lu sniffled as she was wiping her tears away, "Baby, you know I am. More than any words can express! I love you too, baby. God, thank you!"

On the way home, Lu Lu reached in her purse, pulled out a small yellow envelope, and handed it to Bleak. Bleak opened the envelope while inquiring, “Ma, what’s this?” He pulled out a set of keys with a small tag attached to them.

“Just help me find the place. Boy, your guess is as good as mine, so stop asking questions!” Lu lu genuinely had no idea what the keys were for.

The tag read,

S&B Storage Units

2300 Michigan Ave.

(850)434 -1122

Unit 331

As they rode down Michigan Avenue, Bleak spotted the storage company.

"Mama! There it go, right there!" Lu Lu immediately turned into the parking lot.

S&B Storage Units was a small, old looking building that sat close to the highway, with a lot of small storage units located behind it. The units were inside of a ten foot fenced in yard.

Lu Lu and Bleak exited the Chevy, and walked inside the building, to see a young dark-skinned guy, probably in his early thirties, seated behind a counter asleep. Lu Lu tapped the bell on the counter, and the guy jumped up.

"Excuse me; I guess I dozed off, I apologize”…"Now, how can I help y’all today?"

"Yes, “I need to be directed to unit 331.”

"Sure, Ma’am, when the electric gate opens, you can just drive through, and you should see my father”… “He will be able to assist you further, because I really have no idea myself."…"to be honest, I’m just a fill-in!”

“Okay, thank you anyway,” Lu Lu replied kindly with a grin.

Lu Lu and Bleak got back in the car and proceeded through the electric gates. As they reached the back of the storage unit lot, Bleak spotted Unit 331, "Mama, 331, over there."

They exited the car and walked over to it. Lu Lu watched as Bleak stuck the key in the lock.

As he was about to pull the door up, they heard a voice shout.

"Hey! What are y'all doing?"

They both turned to see an old man wearing an overall suit, with a S&B Storage tag on the chest of the uniform. As he walked in their direction he continued,

"Hey! Y'all have a key to that unit?"

Bleak got irritated.

"You see? We got it open!"

The man stared at Bleak as he got closer to him,

"Are you Brad Staples?"

Bleak and Lu Lu looked at one another puzzled, then back at the man, before Lu Lu responded,

"YES HE IS! This is my son, and May I ask Sir, who are you?"

The old man smiled as he removed his hand from his pocket to shake Bleaks hand. Bleak was hesitant at first, but followed the gesture. The man then looked at Lu Lu,

"Hey Luceal , I'm Uncle Sammy!"

Lu Lu immediately rushed over and embraced him with an enormous hug. As tears begun rolling down her face, Lu Lu uttered,

"I been needing to thank you for the money you been sending us all these years... but... but... I...," (he stopped her).

"It's alright Luceal... But It's a Pleasure to final meet y'all!"

Then, he looked over and asked Bleak,

"Lil Man, what are you waiting on? Open it up!"

Bleak pushed the unit door up and couldn't believe his eyes. It was a canary yellow Chevy Caprice Classic with a dark blue rag top. He couldn't help but to blurt out,

"DAM!"

He quickly opened the car door, and saw that the keys were in the ignition. He climbed in and fired it up while mashing down the gas pedal. "Vum Vum," were the sounds the Chevy made, as he riled the engine up.

Sammy had a proud grin on his face.

"Your daddy left this for you"..." I kept it up all these years by keeping it clean and cranking it up from time to time"... "But now, I guess my work is done!".." Enjoy, Son!"..."ENJOY!"

Bleak was stuck, shocked, and amazed all at the same time. After a minute or 2, he got back out of the Chevy, and walked around it, still in disbelief.

Chrome 30 spoke Trues and Vogues, canary yellow leather seats trimmed in blue, and across the back seat stitched in Old English, cursive letters read,

"The legacy Continues."

Bleak continued circling around the car, admiring everything.

"Dam!!"

He uttered again, as he returned back to the driver's side and sat back in the seat.

After sitting for a minute slowly taking it all in, he noticed a tape sticking out the jvc tape deck. He pushed it in while turning up the volume, and the trunk shook as, "Be Good to Me" by the band S.O.S, came bumping through the speaker system.

Bleak sat back, still trying to absorb everything, as he looked through the review mirror, to see Lu Lu and Uncle Sammy walking away talking.

Suddenly Bleak caught a glimpse of a folded piece of paper sticking out of the sun visor. He pulled the visor down and the paper fell right into his lap. It was an envelope addressed to him, so he immediately opened it and begun reading the letter inside.

Bleak,

Son, how are you doing? By this time you should've graduated from high school, so here is my gift to you. The words across the backseat should let you know I've already predicted your future. Son, that's my blood that flows through you, that's my heart that keeps you going...Just promise me you'll be better than I was and do better than I did.

The life I was attempting to live, I did in order, not to have you follow my footsteps, but to make life better for you, and present you with opportunities to see another side, plus travel another route... BUT unfortunately dreams and become nightmares! That's why my life is ending in prison, therefore I can't control your future, nor direct your path, just be better than I was!

And yeah, it wouldn't hurt for you to come see the old man.

Love,

Beankie

P.S. Check the Trunk!

Bleak didn't know how to feel or what to think, because he had never heard anything from his father. He figured Beankie got sentenced life, and since he couldn't be there physically, he forgot about them emotionally as well. That's how Bleak saw it for years, now he felt bad.

Bleak folded up the letter and placed it in the glove compartment, then turned the ignition off, and removed the keys.

He got out of the car and went to the trunk. When he opened the trunk, he saw two 15 inch speakers in a clear plastic speaker box, and a brown bag next to the speakers. He grabbed the bag and opened it, to see it contained three taped up, square shaped blocks.

Bleak removed the keys from the trunk, palmed one of in his hand, and begin sawing on the edge of one the blocks. After sawing back and forth for a few minutes, white powered flakes began drizzling down. Bleak knew what it was, but still tasted the little flakes that fell on his thumb.

"Damn," he whispered to himself as he placed the bag back in the trunk and closed it. Bleak climbed back in the Chevy, fired it up, and backed out of the storage unit.

By that time, Lu Lu and Uncle Sammy were headed back to towards him. Bleak got out and they talked with Uncle Sammy for a few brief moments, then said their cheerful goodbyes.

Lu Lu looked at Bleak

"Baby, I'ma follow you because we need to get your tag and some insurance, before you go driving around town."

"Okay, Ma," Bleak responded.

After they left from getting the tags and insurance situated, they trailed each other home, back to Morris Court.

****

Bleak sat in the car until Lu Lu went into the apartment, then he jumped out and went to the trunk. He grabbed the brown bag, closed the trunk, and ran to Buggaloo's apartment.

Buggaloo was sitting on his front porch when he saw Bleak coming.

"Boy, what you running foe? I thought you were suppose to be graduating today!"

"I did!"

Bleak answered while pulling the brown bag out,

"I just need you to put this up for me. I'll be back later on" ..."and don't go in it!"

Buggaloo grabbed the bag and took it in the house.

As Bleak was running back home, he saw D-Boy, Crash, and Tig standing around the Chevy, observing it, with looks of admiration in their eyes.

"Bleak!" D-Boy yelled,

"I know this ain't you!".

"Yeah, it is!" Bleak replied while walking to where they stood.

"Man, I thought we wasn't copping nothing this yet?" asked Crash.

Tig said nothing, as Bleak replied,

"Man I didn't. My pops gave it to me, well left it for me."

D-Boy shouted out as he took a seat inside the Chevy,

"Man this bitch Clean as a Muthafucker! Shit Nigga lets ride!"

Tig called Bleak to the side,

"Check this out... Man, don't get me wrong, that bitch tight"... I like it, but damn this gon' produce a lot of haters... and you know haters bring HEAT!"..." I thought we were on this low key get money shit!"

Bleak sighed.

"Man I feel you, I get it... But what am I suppose to do? My pops left that for me... People gon' think otherwise....But Fuck em!...And besides that? We all should have at least 6 grand a piece, plus we got about 12 more in the pot...And dope. Shit, it's time to spend a little money! I refuse to ride around the city clean and my click ain't... that won't look right at all"... "We been hustling for two and a half years, only buying clothes and food? Fuck that!"

"Okay... Whatever you say, boss!" Tig retorted in a sarcastic manor.

D-Boy chimed in from the backseat with Crash,

"Man... y'all finished with the wanna-be boss talk?...Cuz, Nigga, We ready to ride!"

Bleak smirked,

"Yeah Nigga, Let's do it!"

They rode for the remainder of the day, from hood to hood, with Master P on repeat. "Only Time Will Tell," playing loudly, they were overwhelmed with the attention the yellow Chevy produced.

The next day they all met up at Buggaloo's apartment, as Bleak had informed them to do the prior night before they parted ways.

As they all gathered around the kitchen table, Bleak whispered for Buggaloo to bring him the bag. Buggaloo hurried to his bedroom and returned with three blocks in his hand. Everyone stared wide-eyed, except for Bleak, as he was shaking his head with a slight smirk.

"Damn Buggaloo, yo nosey ass just had to look in it, huh?"

Buggaloo laughed,

"YES...I ...DID!"..."Look Boy!.. I'm a junky, not a Flunky"... "I smelled coke when your lil ass was running across the parking lot!"

Buggaloo sniffed each packages one by one as he dropped them on the table

"Yeah, these came from Castro. I know his shit from anywhere! Ladies and gentlemen"..."What we have here is grade A cocaine!"

Bleak pushed Buggaloo aside.

"Man, move!"..." You don't know, No Dam Castro!!"

"Yeah ... You right... But I know Dope Thou!"

Crash and D-Boy were stuck just staring at the blocks laying on the table. Tig, in his low key not excited manner, looked at Bleak

"Umm, I guess your pops left you these too, huh?"

Bleak shook his head,

"Yeah!"

Tig continued, "Man, what kind of Daddy you got?"

D-Boy cut in,

"Shit, I'ma answer that dumb ass question!"..."The kind of daddy that's gon' make a your ASS RICH!"... "Case Closed!!. Now, Fuck the who and the why!...Bleak what the is business?"

Bleak wanted to change the subject,

"Yeah right, anyway... we gotta find somebody to cook this shit up. No money owed, more money made."

"Shit, yo man right here," Buggaloo proudly blurted out.

They all looked at him at the same time,

"Buggaloo, you can cook?"

"Nigga, I'm a doctor who never lost a patient... Chef- Loo at your service, and I already bought 10 boxes of baking soda last night!"

Buggaloo spent all night cooking up the blocks of cocaine. Bleak stood watch with him, while D-Boy and Crash sat outside on Buggaloo's back step. While Tig stood posted in Buggaloo's room passing product through the window. Business continued, like a normal day.

****

Buggaloo finished up about 2am in the morning. He had made approximately 144 cookies of crack cocaine using twenty-one grams of cocaine, and 6 grams of baking soda for each cookie. Bleak looked at all of the cookies scattered across the table and on top of the kitchen counter. He looked at Buggaloo, then Crash, while saying.

"Damn... I see why Dow loved us so dam much... Shit, she was getting over big time! ..Nigga, it's gone takes us a year selling dimes and doves!"

They all sat and discussed how they were going to move the drugs faster and agreed on selling weight. All except for Tig, he didn't like the idea.

2 Weeks Later

D-Boy bought a '76 four door Cadillac Sedanville, that he had painted candy purple, with a cream color vinyl top, and matching leather seats. The Cadillac had a gold and chrome grill and sat on all gold 100spoke Dayton rims. On the trunk, D-Boy had an air brushed picture of Morris Ct and Attucks Ct projects, with the words "PRESSURE WORLD," on top, raining $ signs down on the projects.

Crash bought an '84 four door box Chevy. It was Jolly Rancher green, with a dark tan rag top, all gold 100 spoke Dayton rims, and a chrome grill. Crash's seats where dark green with a yellow Polo symbol on the head rest. It was hard as hell, and original.

Tig bought himself an '89 two door thunderbird. It was all black with dark tinted windows. People always mistook it for undercover police car. It was plain, no rims, no loud music, but clean as hell.

****

1 month later.

Bleak came home from shopping, and as he opened the front door, he saw Lu Lu lying passed out on the floor, between the couch and coffee table. He raced over to her in panic and picked her up, placing her on the couch.

“Mama.. Mama, you alright?....Mama!" After she gave no response, he called 911.

After about thirty minutes or so, the ambulance arrived. A crowd of people now stood outside asking questions, as the paramedics entered the apartment, and placed Lu Lu on a stretcher.

“Mama... Say something... Don’t do me like this, mama! I need you!"

Bleak cried on the ride to the hospital, even though the paramedics assured Bleak that everything would be ok.

When they arrived at Baptist Hospital, they exited the ambulance, and rushed Lu Lu into the emergency entrance. Bleak stood beside her as they placed her in a medical bed and hurried to a room. Then, a doctor came to him, advising him to wait in the waiting room until they ran a few tests to figure out what was wrong with Lu Lu.

Bleak resisted, until he heard Lu Lu attempting to say something. The doctor let him enter to hear what it was she was trying to say. As Bleak approached, he asked,

"Mama... You Alright? Talk to me!"

"I'ma be ok baby. Just do what the doctor said, I'll be out in a few."

"Okay, mama, I'll be right out here waiting. Love you!" He kissed her on her forehead and walked off into the lobby.

When Bleak reached the waiting room area, he saw D-Boy, Crash, Tig, and Buggaloo. They walked up to meet him halfway, while asking all at once,

"Man wsup? Lu Lu alright?... What happen?... She alright?”

"Man, I don’t know. She done lost a lil weight and been staying in bed all day long. I kept asking day in and day out, was she ok? She just say she good, just tired... So, I thought nothing of it... But today when I came in, she was passed out on the floor. Man, I hope nothing don’t happen to my mama!"

Bleak’s eyes started to fill with tears, and theirs did also. They all felt like family.

And seeing Bleak in pain, and Lu Lu sick, had them feeling emotional as well. They all sat silently in the waiting room. Then suddenly Bleak looked up and saw Candy and Tasha walking in.

As they made eye contact, Candy rushed over to Bleak and hugged him .

"Is Ms. Lu Lu okay?”

Bleak sighed,

"I'm waiting to see now." Tasha hugged Bleak as well and went over to talk with the D-Boy and the others.

Bleak always had a crush on Candy, but never attempted to make it more than that. Candy knew it because she had a crush on him as well. Even though they hardly said much to one another, they always managed to make eye contact and smile.

Bleak was happy to see her, but he still asked, with a puzzled expression on his face,

"Candy, babe, don’t take this wrong way... But what are you doing here?”

"Showing my concern! Tasha called me and told me something happen... So I went and got her... and here we are!"

Tears began forming in the corners of her eyes, as she rested her head on Bleak’s shoulder.

****

Three hours or so had passed, when they looked up to see Lu Lu. A doctor was pushing her in a wheelchair to where they were seated. Bleak ran up to meet them halfway, "Mama! You okay?"

“I feel better than ever!” Lu Lu smiled while embracing her son.

The doctor turned to Bleak.

“Mr. Staples, are you driving?"

"No, sir, but we have ride.”

The Doctor continued, "Well, Ms. Perkins is ready to go. We ran a few tests and gave her some medication. I will need you to make sure she takes it. I made her an appointment to come back next Monday at 9:30am, can you make sure she will be here?”

"Yes, sir,” Bleak replied.

The doctor finished, "Okay Ms. Perkins, I will see you next Monday. Until then, get some rest, drink plenty fluids, and take the medicine I gave you.”

“I will and thank you!" Lu Lu was ready to leave.

Bleak got behind the wheelchair and pushed Lu Lu over to where everyone else stood. They all hugged Lu Lu, asking her if she was okay. "I'm good, but I will be better if y’all hurry up and get me out of here! I can’t stand hospitals... Especially Baptist!"

D-Boy yelled,

"Okay, Ms. Lu Lu, I’ma go get my car and pull up front!"

Candy laughed, while winking at Lu Lu,

"No D-Boy, I got them!"

Lu Lu agreed, adding, "Yeah, Daryl, Candy got us cuz I seen how you drive! I'll end up back in here for a heart attack!”

They all busted out laughing, as they exited the hospital.

Candy pulled up in front where Bleak and Lu Lu stood. Candy drove a small blue Dodge Neon with dark tinted windows, a car that her mother gave her. The Neon was old looking with a few gray spots where primer had been applied. Candy got out an opened the passenger side door, while asking Bleak if he needed any help getting her in the car. Lu Lu glared at Candy jokingly,

"Girl! I’m pretty sure I can make it! I don’t need y’all grabbing on me like I’m handicap... and better yet? I’m getting in the back so I can stretch out!"

As they drove off Lu Lu said

"Candy, Baby Ms. Lu Lu starving. Do you mind going up to McDonald's? I can sure use a burger and a fudge sundae."

"Sure, Ms. Lu Lu, no problem!"

As they drove, Bleak sat quietly looking out of the window. Candy placed her hand on his lap. When Bleak turned to look at her, she smiled.

"Everything's gon' be alright boo"..."Just have faith."

Bleak peeked back at Lu Lu and she was nodding her head as if saying,

"Fool, you better make your move... say something!" Bleak grinned because he could read his mother's thoughts. He looked back over at Candy,

"How come you're so friendly all of a sudden? We hardly ever spoke in the hood or at school before you moved. Now we friends? Not mad, just confused."

Candy looked in her review mirror and Lu Lu met her eyes.

"Well Brad, I never had a chance to..." she trailed off.

Lu Lu giggled at them both.

"Y'all kids crazy. Just stop beating around the bush and beat the bush! Y'all like each other and been liking each other. Life's too short to miss out on what could be... I know that from experience!"

Bleak just shook his head, but he had a big smile on his face.

When they arrived at McDonald's, Candy parked because Bleak wanted to use the restroom. He asked Candy if she wanted anything to eat before he went inside.

"Yeah Baby, I want whatever Ms. Lu Lu having," she answered with a wink.

"Okay!" Bleak got out and headed inside McDonald's.

As soon as Bleak was far enough that he couldn't hear, Candy and Lu Lu started talking, Lu Lu first.

"Oh Girl!...You trying to halla at, My Lil Baby?"

"Yeah, Ms. Lu Lu... Me and Bleak been liking each other since the ninth grade... But... Well... I guess both of us was too shy to make the first move. So now, I'm taking the initiative."

Lu Lu, thrilled with Candy's response.

"Okay, you go girl, I hear you! And, Bleak needs a good a woman in his life"..."and to be honest, girl, I think that boy still a virgin!"

"Ms. Lu Lu!" Candy interrupted, shocked but laughing at Lu Lu words.

Lu Lu went on with a chuckle,

"Girl, I'm just being honest, that's my baby!" They both laughed, at the same time Bleak was approaching the car.

Bleak opened the door and slowly got in, while staring at them both,

"Really?...The car was shaking too hard for y'all to be looking innocent right now. I know y'all were talking about me!"..." Don't stop now, carry on."

Candy was laughing even harder now,

Boy, ain't nobody talking 'bout you!"

When they got back to Morris Court, Candy parked in front of Lu Lu's apartment. Lu Lu got out of the car and looked at Candy.

"Thank you, my future daughter-in-law, talk to you later!"

"Oh, most definitely! I'll be over tomorrow to check up on you."

After Lu Lu went into their apartment, Bleak sat in silence for a moment then asked,

"So!"...What now? You coming in?"

"No... but I will be back tomorrow to check up on y'all."

"Oh, okay,"..."So, my next question is... wsup wit you?"

"Bleak... What you mean by that?" Candy asked, with a coy grin.

Bleak laughed

"I'm talking about this... all of a sudden attention I'm getting from you!"

"Well Bleak, I was just trying to show my concern and be a friend."

"Friend huh... and what if I want to be more?"

Candy giggled,

"Bleak, you had your chance but you was scared to follow up."

Bleak, looked into Candy's eyes before getting out of the car.

"Well, with me it's always better late than never!"

He closed her passenger door and headed towards his apartment. Candy rolled down her window.

"So what you mean about that?"

Bleak shrugged,

"I guess it'll come to you. When you're ready to stop playing, let me know!"

Then he went in the apartment and closed the door.

Inside the apartment yelled out.

"Mama"..."Where you at?"

"I'm in my room."

Bleak walked to the door, knocked, then went in. Lu Lu was sitting up on her bed, reading a letter, with a shoe box full of letters sitting in her lap. Bleak sat down beside her, "Mama, what you reading?"

"A letter from your daddy."

"From my daddy? He wrote you?" Bleak was shocked and confused.

"Yeah baby, all the time!" She passed Bleak the shoe box, "Ha... See for yourself."

Bleak grabbed the box and opened it, to see that it contained a bunch of cards and letters addressed to Lu Lu. Bleak looked back at Lu Lu, "Ma, you mean to tell me you and my daddy been keeping contact all these years, and nobody said nothing to me? That's foul!"

"Baby that's how your daddy wanted it. He didn't want you to know. Why? Beats me, but he always wrote and still writes. He sends cards on your birthdays and all."

Bleak pulled one of the cards out of the box and begin reading it.

Lu Lu

What's up baby? I can't begin to explain how sorry I am to have left you with the burden of having to raise our son alone. Today is his 9th birthday... Wow. How is he doing?

I see he done got taller. I place all of his pictures you send in my photo album from year to year to see how he is developing into becoming a man.

Well baby I love y'all and remember what I say in every letter about sharing my emotions. Because I'm stuck in this hell for life and my heart can't bare the pain of not being there to share these special moments...and I don't need his heart in here worrying about me. I'm waiting until he is all grown up.

Anyhow baby, I'll write you again in 3 months as usual.

Love You

Beankie

As Bleak placed the card on the bed he thought to himself,

"All this time I thought my pops didn't give a damn about us... since he couldn't be here physically, he forgot about us emotionally as well. I guess he been in the shadows all along, all these years."

He looked at Lu Lu, trying not to show any emotion.

“Mama, I need to go see him.”

Lu Lu nodded her head in agreement and said,

"I think so too, baby."

Six days later

Lu Lu woke Bleak up,

"Bleak, boy, get up!”...” Daryl wild ass out there with that loud music turned up sky high."

Bleak got up and threw on some clothes. When he got outside, D-Boy was sitting on the hood of his ‘76 Deville,

"Bleak! Wsup Boy?”...”We got about forty-nine of them thangs left and I’m finna go sell six of ‘em to cats over East. Then, I’m finta to put the ‘lac up!”

Bleak tried to hide a laugh,

"Boy, you wild! And you finta put the ‘lac up where?"

"IN THE AIR!...Nigga!" D-Boy continued, "Nigga I’m getting switches on this Bitch!"...”Pressure world to the fullest!...Nigga!”

Bleak couldn’t hold it in this time, and he shook his head laughing.

D-Boy was being dead serious,

"Ride with your boy!”...” I’ma go serve these cats over East, then drop the ‘lac off at CA Customs”... “We'll catch a cab back, cuz I don’t want nobody to know shit.. ‘til I come through this bitch on three wheels!"

Bleak hopped in, still laughing at D-Boy.

As they rode, Bleak turned down the music to ask about business.

"So, y'all got about forty-nine of them thangs left?"

"Yeah, forty-three when I off these six. You had suggested we start selling weight and these shits been flying like Frisbees"... "Me and Crash been popping $1000 an circle"..." Tig and Buggaloo have been still serving 20's and shit...but most of the time Buggaloo be solo, still coming clean with the whole $1000"..." We got about seventy grand in the pot and you know Grandma holding that down...and Tig got about six or seven grand on standby for you!"

D-Boy paused to laugh

"Man, you know he call himself running shit...Well both u niggas think that"..."but since you been tending to Lu Lu... this Nigga Be Tripping!... he be acting like me and Crash hot or something."

"Oh yeah,"

Bleak replied with a smirk on his face. Tig had already informed him about how D-Boy and Crash had been clowning around the city, throwing up stacks of money in the club and having stripper parties at expensive hotels. Now with D-Boy about to get switches on the Cadillac, he knew what Tig was talking about, but it didn't bother him one way or the other. In his mind, they were finally getting money and why not enjoy it? They all grew up from nothing with nothing.

Bleak uttered out loud, "I'ma get my Mama out the projects!"

"I feel you dog... But as for me? The Hill is home... My grandma would die anywhere else!"

D-Boy paused for a second,

"oh yeah, you know I been messin' around with Tasha... She been dreaming about moving in together, but it ain't nothing!"..."Anyway!...Wsup with you and Candy? I overheard her and Tasha talking about you. Dog, you need to be getting that! Tasha bad, but Candy? Damn! That pecan tan skin, with that long natural hair, none of that weave shit, that small fat lil round ass...and belly ring game going on... Shit, nigga you slipping, plus she going to school to be a veterinarian?.... Nigga, you better get your shots!"...Before one these worms get u!"

Bleak could only laugh more,

"Boy, you crazy."

"Crazy? Ha! ...Nigga you better get your shots...And tell me about it!."

As they reached the East side of town, they turned off 9th Avenue, rode a few blocks down, they made a right, then stopped at a brown brick house halfway down the block they turned on to.

D-Boy hit the horn, and shortly after, four dudes came outside. D-Boy got out and talked to them. One of the dudes saw Bleak sitting in the car.

"Bleak! Wsup Boy?"

"Chillin' Homie," Bleak replied.

Then, D-Boy and the four dudes walked around to back of the house. About ten minutes went by before D-Boy returned with a brown paper bag in his hand. He then got back in the car and they drove off .They turned a few corners around the East side of town with the music bumping.

As they paused at a stop sign, a car behind them ran into the ass end of D-Boy's Cadillac. D-Boy immediately through the 'lac in park and got out.

"What the fuck!"..."O Hell No!"

As he got to the back of his car to look at the damage, he motioned for the occupants to get out of what appeared to be, a black Nissan Maxima, with dark tinted windows. D-Boy couldn't see who was in it, so he approached it. As he did, the driver's side window came slightly down, and the barrel of a pistol pointed out quickly. D-Boy tried to turn and run back towards his car.

"SHIT!"

Bleak turned around to see what was going on.

"POW, POW, POW, POW!"

Was the sounds he heard as he saw fire spitting out of the car and D-Boy stumbling trying to make it back to the lac.

Bleak immediately jumped in the driver's seat while trying to open the back door, but by that time, the guys were out of the Maxima, walking towards the car, still busting shots. Bleak had no choice but to put the car in drive and pull off. As he went a short distance up the street, he made hard u-turn, heading back in their direction.

When they saw the 'lac coming back at them in full speed, they jumped back in the Maxima, and tried to avoid a head on collision by swerving to the left. However, Bleak managed to catch the tail end of the Maxima, which made it do a complete 180. Bleak peeped over to see D-Boy laying on the curb, covered in blood, then he looked in the review to see what the car was doing. He wasn't taking any chances, so he threw the 'lac in reverse and speed backwards. The other car did the same, then yoked around and took off up the street.

Bleak stopped where D-Boy was laying, then jumped out and grabbed him, attempting to lay him across the back seat.

"Hold on homie, I got you! Damn, I got you! This shit can't be happening!"

Bleak was crying as he said the words to assure D-Boy. Bleak closed the door and took off.

"I'ma get you to the hospital... Hold on homie."

Bleak only got a few blocks up the street as he saw police cruisers came from every Direction. As they surround the car, with guns drawn. Bleak got out of the car with his hands in the air.

"My friend shot, he need an ambulance."

The Police officers yelled .

"Get down, Get down", as Bleak got on the ground he kept uttering.

"Man, My friend need an Ambulance...he been shot."

The officers ran up to him and grabbed his hand while placing cuffs on them and other officers were at the Cadillac, one yelled

"We got a man down over here",

Bleak replied,

"I just told you Muthafuckas that... while ya'll hand cuffing me, my man could be dying!!"

An officer placed him in the back seat of one of the 8 police cruisers that arrived on the scene, and then shut the door.

Bleaks' mind was racing, all he thought about was D-Boy and how it would be the officer's fault if D-Boy died. Tears began rolling down his face. Then he saw the ambulance, and the paramedics jumped out with a stretcher and placed D-Boy on it and quickly took off. Now while the police officers proceeded to search the car, one of the officers motioned for the others to come over. Then Bleak saw the brown paper bag in the officer's hand, he thought to himself that was the bag that D-Boy had placed the money in.

The officers had talked for a few minutes, and then 2 unmarked cars pulled up. One of the officers in the unmarked car went over to where the other officers stood, they showed him the bag as they all talked, and then one pointed at the patrol car that Bleak was seated in, hand cuffed. The officer that got out of the unmarked vehicle had approached the cruiser Bleak was in and opened the door,

"Hey Son...Are you alright?"

"Yah, when ya'll get these damn cuffs off me, for I can go to the hospital and check on my friend."

The officer replied (as he kneeled down to talk),

"Well Son, take it easy, I just got a few questions for you...and first off my name is SGT. Matthews and yours?"

"Brad Staples," SGT. Matthews continued,

"Alright Mr. Staples, what is your friend's name?"

"Daryl Wiggins,"

"Mr. Wiggins,"

SGT. Matthews repeated as he took a small notebook pad out of his top left shirt pocket, then he continued asking questions.

"Mr. Staples, what happened here today? Was somebody trying to rob you or Mr. Wiggins?"

"No Man," Bleak said with an attitude then continued,

"We were just riding and a small blue car pulled up on us and went to shooting."

"A small blue car," SGT. Matthews confirmed, and then responded.

"Witness claim it was Black Maxima!"

"Black, Blue, Yellow, MAN, why am I sitting here hand cuffed?"

SGT. Matthews answered.

"First of all, Mr. Staples, this is a regular procedure, we have to find what happened in cases like these and on top of that, you're not being any real help...You say that's your friend, but you are lying about what color car the people who shot him were driving, plus we find $4,000 dollars and an ounce of crack cocaine in the Cadillac you or your friend was driving, but when officers arrived, you were found behind the wheel. Now let me ask you again, did somebody try to rob ya'll or do you know who was shooting at ya'll and what for?"

Bleak shook his head.

"Man I just want to go check on my homeboy; Fuck the rest of this shit!"

SGT. Matthews then stood up straight and closed his note pad.

"Well you just hold on for a few minutes, Mr. Staples," then he closed the door.

Bleak was hot, not knowing was D-Bo alright plus at all the shit that was going on with the Police.

SGT. Matthews went back over to where the other officers stood and proceeded talking to another undercover officer that was in the other unmarked car, who was dressed in plain clothes, they looked over in Bleaks' direction as they talked, and then the other officer in plain clothes came over an opened the door. When he opened the door of the cruiser Bleak was seated. He looked at Bleak face to face for a second then asked.

"You, Brad Staples?"

"Yah Man,"

"What's your Mother's name?"

"Luceal Perkins!"

"What's your Father's name?"

"Man"..."I'm adopted."

The officer then turned around and yelled for SGT. Matthews.

As SGT. Matthews got to the car he asked.

"What's up, Danny? Is he talking now?,"

"NO, He Ain't talking!"... BUT, do you know whose Son this is?"

"No!"... I didn't ask."

Danny then continued,

"This is Benjamin Staples's boy, aka Beankie!"

SGT. Matthews face turned fire red. Bleak just looked off he didn't know where this was going, but from the look of things, It wasn't good.

Then Danny, who's whole name was "Danny Bernard", went on talking.

"You see Brad, I'm old school, I been working on the force for 23 years...Now SGT. Matthews, on the other hand he's sort of new"..." he's only been on the force for 7 years"…" but he always wanted to be a Police officer, mainly because his father was one"…" in which, I've had the pleasure to serve with once upon a time"…" You see me and Matt's father use to assist the FEDS with Narcotics Operations…. "But anyways…. to make a long story short, I want to take this opportunity to introduce ya'll"… "Brad Staples, this is SGT. Mike Matthews, son of James J. Matthews, the officer your low life father killed."

Bleak just dropped his head and SGT. Matthews slammed the door and walked off, with Danny a few steps behind.

After an hour had passed, an officer had got in the car and pulled off. Bleak had his eyes closed, until he felt the car moving. Bleak arose. "Hey Man, Where we going?"

"To Jail," replied the officer.

Bleak was in disbelief.

"Nigga!"…"FOR WHAT?"

The officer then stated.

"They are charging you with possession of crack cocaine with intent to distribute."

Bleak leaned back into the seat, not fully accepting what was happening.

As they pulled into the Sally Port of the Escambia County Jail, the officer exited the vehicle and got him out of the backseat. As they walked through the electric doors, the officer told Bleak,

"Since you'll be 18 years old within a few weeks or so, they gon charge you as an adult, so the good thing about it, you can bond out. Your bond is $10,000 cash or professional, which is $1,000 dollars to a bondsman".

Then after a pause, the officer continued,

"Son, I'm just doing my job, but to me this whole situation fucked up, but I'ma try to get you booked in quickly, for you can use the phone and check up on your friend."

"Thank you," Bleak replied as the officer took the cuffs off.

Meanwhile at the Pensacola Police Station, SGT. Matthews and Lt. Danny Bernard sat around a table with 3 other Narcotic officers and a crime scene investigator.

One of the Narcotics Officers stood up and began speaking,

"Gentleman today was another tragedy. I say that every time a young man is murdered due to drugs and violence."

He paused to open up a folder that contained photos.

"This is our victim (the picture he handed around the table was of D-Boy) (as the photo went from hand to hand the officer continued) this is Daryl Wiggins our deceased, aka D-Boy and as most of us know this is Ms. Anna Bell's grandson. We've been hearing a lot about this boy as well as these other 2 boys on the photos I'm fixing to pass around. Now the 2 cd one is Edwin Dees aka Crash and the last but not least is this one Brad Staples, aka Bleak, the one you arrested today. Now all these boys reside in the Morris Court Projects and they have been making a pretty lil penny lately right under our noses. In the last few weeks they done purchased cars and God knows what else, but we got nothing on them as of this moment, but they are on the rise. At this time, I would like to introduce and join the legendary Danny Bernard, along with SGT. Matthews to this investigation, cause how I see it Gentleman, if we don't get in the middle, we are going to have a little war on the streets cause these 2 boys ain't gone lay down. I know that much about 'em. And Brad Staples Father is the low thug that killed SGT. Matthews's Father, James Matthews who was a part of this department and specialized in taking drug dealers down and putting them where they belong."

Danny stood up then and said,

"Yah, Me and James go way back and I feel delighted to be a part of this investigation, I'ma lil old, but not rusty. I know these streets like the back of my hands."

The other officers stood up as well and clapped, and then they all shook hands.

As the officers walked out of the room Danny turned towards SGT. Matthews.

"Cheer up son, I know you miss your old man."

"It's not only that Danny, after you informed me of who's son it was, I felt like doing something out of my position, out of character, I felt like getting revenge. When I first joined the force, I wanted to take down every low life thug out there and break the rules if I had to, but as I got older I got more into my job. I live"..." to live by the book"... "And not seek revenge, or use this badge for other purposes!"..."Now that I think about it... I was wrong for how I felt, because that young man isn't responsible for my Father's death."

Danny then cut him off,

"So you feel sympathy for a young dope dealer, who's Father, killed yours in cold blood?"

"No!"..."Absolutely Not!"..."I'ma just, play by the rules!"

Danny smirked.

"I'm not breaking any rules Son, we gone get 'em fair and square"..." then I'ma break all the rules"..." before I put him in the cell next to his Father!"..." Now let's ride Son"... "I got informants to dig up!"... "That's if they're still living!"

BACK IN JAIL

After Bleak got searched and they counted the money that he had on him, which was only $15 dollars, they handed him a pink confiscation slip for $4,000 dollars and let him go inside to use the phone.

As he got in the lobby, he saw people sleeping, talking, and crying, and so on. He grabbed a phone, but then a girl on another phone next to him said,

"You got to use this one, it calls straight out, the other ones, you need a pin number to use. I'll be off in a minute."

Shortly after, she passed him the phone.

Bleak called Buggaloo's house, Tig picked up the phone on the first ring,

"Hello, hello!"

"Man, I'm in jail, I need you to come bond me out and Hurry up!"

Tig asked,

"Man you ain't heard about D-Boy!"

"Yah, man come get me, I need to get to the Hospital."

Tig yelled in the phone in a shaky voice,

"Dog!" Bleak?...D-Boy Dead!!!"

Bleak hung up the phone, and then leaned against it while facing the wall and began crying.

After 15 minutes or so passed, he suddenly felt someone tapping on his shoulder; he then turned around while wiping the tears away from his eyes and was face to face with some tall, dark skinned dude.

"Homie, could somebody else use the phone?"

The dude said with authority, while exposing his gold teeth.

Bleak clicked, he grabbed the phone receiver with his right hand and grabbed the tall dude's shirt collar with his left hand and quickly began beating him in the face and head with the phone receiver. C.O.'s started coming from every direction. They pushed the tall dude out the way and grabbed Bleak. Bleak let go of the phone, as they began dragging him off.

They placed in a holding cell alone and as he sat, he couldn't digest all that has happened. He felt somewhat responsible of what happened to D-Boy

"Only if I would have grabbed him earlier"…" or if I didn't stop for the Police and pushed it all the way to hospital."

The more he thought about it, the madder at himself he became.

He sat in the cell for about 2 ½ hours, and then suddenly he heard his name being called,

"Brad Staples."

Bleak ran to the cell door.

"Yah, I'm back here."

Then a short old lady came to the door, dressed in a county jail employee uniform with a C.O. in front of her. The C.O. opened the door and stood between Brad and the old lady as she asked him

"Mr. Stamples, is it safe to take you out of there?"

"Yes Ma'ma!"

"Okay Sir...your bondsman is here, and as soon as your finger printed and get your picture taken ... you can go."

"Yes Ma'am!"

The officer motioned for him to come out.

While Bleak was getting finger printed the C.O. said

"You lucky that boy didn't press charges,"

Bleak ignored the comment.

After he was finger printed he went to a glass window to talk to the Bondsman. The Bondsman's name was "Sonny Reese". Sonny Reese was a stocky white guy with dark black hair. He had on a black shirt with Sonny Reese Bail Bonds written in yellow print across his chest. He talked as Bleak listened and signed his name on some papers, then he was released.

When he got into the lobby Lu Lu, Tig, Crash, Buggaloo, Tasha, Ms. Anna Bell and Candy all stood waiting. They all approached him with hugs and he could tell that they all had been crying. Bleak immediately went back over to Ms. Anna Bell.

"Ms. Anna Bell I'm sorry," as tears ran down his and her faces.

"I know Baby. I heard about what happened...you tried to save him."

They continued hugging each other, and then Lulu said in a low tone,

"Ya'll let's get out of here."

Outside Bleak and Lulu got in the car with Candy after Bleak helped Tig put Ms. Anna Bell back in Tig's car and Buggaloo got in the car with Crash. Tasha rode alone.

They all trailed each other back to Morris Court Projects.

As they pulled in, they saw people standing outside of Ms. Anna Bell's apartment. Everybody was looking sad and upset all at the same time. As Tig pulled up someone opened the door for Ms. Anna Bell while, Tig went to the trunk to retrieve her wheel chair.

Nobody could believe that D-Boy was dead. Everyone just sat around silent and teary eyed.

After hours passed, people began to return to their apartments. Ms. Anna Bell told the people that was seated in her living room that she wanted to be alone. So they also began leaving, Bleak stood to kiss her on the cheek before he left and she pulled him close and whispered,

"Stay here for a second I need to talk to you."

Lulu told Bleak,

"I'll be at home Baby," as she hugged Ms. Anna Bell and left.

Crash, Tig, Buggaloo, Tasha and Candy along with a few others did the same.

Bleak told Candy before she walked out of the apartment, to wait for him.

When the house was cleared, Ms. Anna Bell looked at Bleak.

"Baby all I want is the Muthafuckas responsible...DEAD!!"..."We clear?"

Bleak just nodded his head, because in his mind that was mandatory, but now with Ms. Anna Bell saying it, it was official..

Ms. Anna Bell continued,

"I know you gone do it anyway, but I want to look em in the eyes before they die"..." I want to see em die"..."not just hear about it!"

Bleak nodded, then she finished.

"I love you Baby," as she continued wiping the tears away from her eyes.

Bleak turned to walk out the door, but before doing so she said,

"I'ma still continue to hold the money!"..."But all I want... is to look that muthafucka in his eyes!...as he take his last breathe!"

"You will Ms. Anna Bell" ..."I promise you!,"

Bleak walked out the door and got in the car with Candy.

As Bleak sat in silence in the passenger seat, Candy asked him,

"Baby, You alright?"

"I will be!"

Candy continued,

"Damn, what ya'll doing?"..."I mean when we were all going to school, ya'll wasn't carrying on like this!"

Suddenly she began crying as she continued.

"Dam, and Tasha was just talking about, they were finta get them a place together" ..."and she pregnant!!"..." but he ain't get a chance to find out!"..."Man, this shit is all fucked up!!"

As they were leaving out of the projects, Bleak told her to stop where he saw Tig and Crash standing. Bleak climbed out and went over to talk to Tig, after a few seconds Tig handed Bleak some money out of his pocket. While telling Bleak,

"I'll watch out for Lulu while you gone." Bleak got back in the car with Candy and they pulled off.

As they rode for 30 minutes or so in complete silence, Bleak then asked,

"You said Tasha was pregnant?"

"Yah," Candy replied.

"Does Ms. Anna Bell know?"

"You know Ms. Anna Bell know everything...You don't have to tell her nothing," and in that very moment for the first time in hours Bleak smiled.

"You, hungry?"

"I could use a lil something!"

So they both agreed on Red Lobster Seafood which was in front of Cordova Mall.

After they ate and talked, they walked out and got back into the car. Candy asked,

"So, where too, now?"

"Residence Inn!"

She looked at him, while starting up the Neon, but said nothing.

She then got on the highway and headed to the Residence Inn, she remembered seeing it, on their way to Red Lobster.

As she pulled into the entrance he got out and went in to get a room. When he came back and got in the car. Candy said

"Baby, I need to go by my house!"..."Are you going with me?"

"Yah, I guess so,"

When they reached Candy's house, she pulled into the driveway and exited the vehicle, while Bleak sat in the car.

Shortly after, she returned with a back pack and tossed it into the back seat, as she got back in the car.

"Dam C, I see you and your family been doing good since ya'll moved out of the projects, Huh?"...And you fin-ta be a Veterinarian? Right?,"

Caddy looked over at him as she turned the car back on and pulled off. She figured to herself that Tasha told D-Boy and D-Boy told Bleak, but she didn't want to mention that at the moment, considering the fact that D-Boy was dead.

As they got to the hotel, they parked and exited the car, she grabbed her back pack and then they both entered the lobby of the hotel, there she followed Bleak toward the elevator. Candy admired the scenery; there was big, colorful, exotic plants everywhere that matched the purple, red and green carpet and wall paper. There were brass picture frames, with outdoor paintings such as mountains, plants and different types of animals. When the elevator opened, they entered. Bleak pulled the hotel card key out of his pocket to make sure what the room number was and what floor it was on, then pushed the 4th floor button.

When elevator stopped, the doors opened smoothly. Bleak said,

"It's room 224."

As they got out they saw arrows pointing in different directions and they followed the one that read 200-250.

When they suddenly, approached room 224, Bleak placed the card in the slot.

As they entered, Candy turned to look at Bleak, as he closed the door and turned on the lights. She then turned back around, to over look what she saw.

"Wow...This must be a Presidential Suite!"

She saw a living room and a full kitchen. She walked over to some sliding doors and opened them to see a bedroom with a bathroom in it, then looked in the bathroom and saw a Jacuzzi in the middle of the floor.

As Caddy looked around Bleak, sat on the couch and turned on the TV.

Caddy then came and sat beside him, while leaning her head on his shoulder

"Baby, you need to calm down"..." I know a lot of shit going through your mind right now"..." but don't lose focus, just relax!"..." and remember ...I'm suffering too!!"

She got up and went back into the bedroom.

A few minutes later, Bleak heard the water running and he assumed she was bathing, so he stretched out on the couch.

He began thinking about all the events that occurred, in such a short period of time:

His Pops left him a car and 3 bricks ...and he hasn't thanked him or nothing.

Lulu fell out and he had to rush her to the hospital.

He had been shot at.

D-Boy dead and plus, he went to jail.

Life seemed fucked up at the moment.

Then he thought about Lulu's doctor appointment, which was tomorrow.

He snapped out of the fucked up mind state he was in, when he heard Candy yell, "Bleak, Bleak, come in here."

He then got up and walked into the room and entered the bathroom to see her laying in the Jacuzzi. She splashed some water on him as he stood in the door way.

"You not getting in?"

After a minute or two, he took off his clothes and climbed in with her, she stood as he sat down, then she came and sat in front of him as if sitting on his lap with her head laying back against his chest.

Caddy turned around to look at him

"Baby, you got to calm down," as she began kissing him passionately.

She felt his manhood stiffen up, as she grabbed it with her left hand (while still tonguing him) and then slowly slid it in her.

As she began slowly, sliding up and down on it, feeling its full length. She began to moan,

"AHHHHHHH..AHHH, Baby", as her moans got louder.

Bleak wrapped his arms around her waist and pushed himself in and out as she came up and down increasing her momentum with every thrust. All he could do was keep his eyes closed and enjoy the warm feeling.

After a 20 minutes or so Candy moaned even louder and then it turned into a whisper

"O'Baby, I'm Cumming...Dam, I'm Cumming,"..." Shit, I'm so wet...Baby, Dam I believe I squirted...Lord-ham- Mercy!!"...." Boy u gone make me go Crazy! "

"Shush, Baby let's get in the bed." Bleak whispered.

Then they got out of the Jacuzzi, with their bodies still soak and wet. Caddy pushed him on the bed and they made love for the remainder of the night.

The next morning he woke up and looked to his side and Candy wasn't there. He then climbed out of bed, and looked at the clock on the TV and saw that it was 10:40am; he grabbed the phone and called home, but received no answer so he assumed that Lulu had made her appointment.

CHAPTER 3

"Hey Crash...wake your ass up,"

Dow yelled (Crash's Auntie).

"Hey Crash,"

She yelled out again.

As she saw him slowly raised up, and became fully focused.

To his surprise he saw Dow standing in the door way entrance to his room.

(Dow was short, she stood about 5'2, she had a nice shape, but was real dark and ugly, and she wore long dreadlocks that stayed wrapped around the top of her head. She wore a lot gold as well, which supported her facial features, plus she had a mouth full of gold. She always wore jeans and sneakers and if she wasn't married, you would mistake her for being a dyke cause that's how she carried herself. Dow was Haitian/Black American but had a deep New Orleans accent.)

She continued after she saw that he was fully aware of her presence,

"Luk boy!"...."You'll be dodging me... I risk me life, to bring ya'll stuff and ya'll nowhere to be find!"..." I hear bout friend"..."Me sorry.... but me not feel bad!"..."Cuz where I stay... it Happen daily!"

Crash jumped up with anger

"That's My Dam Dog, Brother, Friend, and Homie that died...What the fuck you mean bout you don't feel bad...Man, Fuck you...And the reason we ain't been halla'n at your ass.... because you had been getting over all along, Bitch."

Crash mother rushed in the room.

"What the hell going on Boy? What you talking to your Auntie like that for?"

Crash grabbed a shirt to put on out of his closet while replying,

"Ask her?"..."O, my bad!"..."I forgot!" ..."she bring ya'll a lil dope, so you'll treat her like a Queen...Man, I'm outta here!"

Crash walked out of the house and jumped into his box Chevy and pulled off.

He stopped by Tig's house and got out to knock on the door. Tig's Mother answered and told him that Tig wasn't there, so Crash got back in the car and went to Buggaloo's house. He then got out and walked in.

As he entered he saw Tig & Buggaloo along with 2 other men. Tig yelled from in the kitchen.

"Crash... come see what you want!"

As Crash got to the kitchen table, he looked down and saw guns scattered around the table: 3.9 millimeters, 2 380's, 1 Tex 9 semi automatic and what appeared to be a pistol grip shot gun. He immediately grabbed the shot gun.

"This is what I need RIGHT HERE!"..."For I can go Blow the Doors...off My Auntie Shit!"

Buggaloo and Tig looked at each other before grabbing the shot gun out of his hand. Tig then turned to the 2 guys,

"What you want for everything?"...

The 2 men talk among one another for a second then said 5 grand and that includes 3 extra clips with the 9's and 380's plus blunts and 1 box of shells for the riot pump." Crash asked

"Why you call it a riot pump?"

One of the men explained as he demonstrated with the pump shot gun in his hand,

"It shoots 10 shells – It's good for crowds."

Tig then paid the gentlemen and they left.

After the men left Crash immediately inquired

"Man we need find out who killed D-Boy!"

"Man I got people on it, I put 5000 for any reliable info"..."Plus Attuck Ct, want they ass too"..."but regardless"... "when find out, we gon wait and see how Bleak want to handle it.".." D-Boy funeral next Saturday, so we gon continue hustling...no serving niggas...we back to 10's and 20's... that serving shit out! ..."cause what it boils down to...like it or not, that's what got D-Boy killed and Bleak in jail. I didn't like the idea to begin with, I like to keep it hood."

Lulu arrived at Baptist Hospital 10 minutes after 9. As she got out of the car, she told Candy,

"Thanks you, Baby," and headed towards the Hospital's entrance.

"Ms Lu Lu, You don't want me to go in with you?"

Lulu turned around.

"Baby, I'll be alright"…" you just go back take care of my Boy," Caddy smiled as she waved Bye to Lulu, then pulled off.

Lulu walked into the Hospital's cafeteria to get a bite to eat, since she had 20 minutes left until her appointment, she ordered a sausage, grits and eggs combo that came with toast and large drink, in which she got orange juice.

When she got her food, she looked around to find an empty table to eat at. After she finished her food, she looked up at the clock on the wall and saw that it was now 9:25am, so she walked over to the trash can and threw the disposable dishes away, and head to the elevator. She always felt uncomfortable at Hospitals and the last time she had been was when she had Bleak, which was now 18 years ago. She replayed that day in her mind, as she rode in the elevator to the 5th floor, but came back to reality when the elevator stopped and the doors immediately opened. She exited and went to a desk where a young pretty white female was seated behind.

"Good morning Ma'am, and how may I assist you today?"

"Good morning to you as well"…, "I am here to see Dr. Fazora and my name is Luceal Perkins."

The secretary looked at her appointment log, the passed Lulu a clip board with some forms attached to it.

"Here you go Ms. Perkins, just have a seat and fill these papers out, Dr. Fazora will be with you in a minute,"

Lulu replied "Thank you," as the secretary responded with a smile.

Lulu looked around the small waiting room, before sitting down beside a heavy set Hispanic lady, with 3 uncontrollable boys. The lady spoke,

"Hi you do!" as Lulu sat down.

"Girl, I'ma make it!"…" How about yourself?"

The Hispanic lady looked at her 3 lil boys as they ran around the little office, then looked back at Lulu

"You take them and then I'll be alright."

Lulu smile

"Baby"..."I got 1 and he was more than enough for me," the lady laughed, while Lulu placed the clip board in her lap and began filling out the papers.

After 30 minutes passed, a Doctor came out a door beside the desk where the secretary sat and asked, "Do I have a Luceal Perkins?" Lulu stood and walked over towards him, then the Doctor said, "Hi, Ms. Perkins, You feeling alright?"

"Better than ever!", then he motioned for her to follow him through the door, in which he came out of.

They then entered a small room and she sat in a chair next a desk where he sat also, he then rolled up her sleeve and checked her pulse and blood pressure. He wrote the reading in a folder. Then Lulu asked him,

"Is everything alright?"

Dr. Fazora removed his glasses

"Ms. Perkins I have bad news."

Lulu's heart dropped as she asked, "What is it?"

Dr. Fazora replied, "Ms. Perkins, you've been diagnosed with being HIV Positive." Lulu stood up

"WHAT???"

"Yes, Ms. Perkins you have the Retro virus that causes AIDS, but with the proper medication you could still manage to live a long time, but that part is up to you."

Lulu screamed, "Lord, what have I done...Please Lord tell me what I have done, what's going on?" Then she began crying uncontrollably.

"Ms. Perkins, I'm give you a minute alone…I can't imagine how you feel, but I have seen a lot of these situations so just sit while I fill you out a prescription. You'll have to go to the Health Department Clinic, where they will have some questions for you, along with some forms to fill out, Ms. Perkins I'm Sorry!"

Lulu didn't hear a word he said, she just kept crying. After he left out of the office, he returned and said,

"I'll make you out a lil map so you wouldn't have no problem finding what desk you should report to, as I said Ms. Perkins, I'm sorry."

Caddy pulled up in the driveway of her Mother's house, in which she lived also. The house was upstairs and downstairs, with light blue vinyl siding. The driveway had a large car porch where 2 cars could be parked in at one time. It had a mini sized garden that surrounded the front porch. It had a small front yard and a side walk that lead from the entrance of the car porch to the front door and also from the front door to the side walk where people traveled. It had a big back yard, enclosed in a fence that began on the right side of the house and ended at the car porch on the left side of the house. Inside of the car porch was a side door and when you entered you would be in the kitchen area of the house.

Caddy exited the Neon directly under the car porch and saw the side door open. As she walked in her step Father was seated at the kitchen table, "Good Morning," he said.

"Good Morning," Caddy replied then he continued,

"I used to be able to tell you Good night, but I guess you heard that from someone else, huh?"… "Caddice look here, I know you're becoming a woman but at least be a child and tell me your mother something!"…"Especially, if you're not planning on coming home."

"I'm sorry, Bow Bow."

(Bow Bow, whose real name was Jesse Smith, had married Caddy's Mother, whose name was Jacqueline Stallworth, now Jacqueline Smith, but everyone called her Jackie – Bow Bow was a hard working man, he moved Jackie and Caddy out of the projects after they had got married, they only dated 5 months before he proposed and she excepted. Bow Bow was tall, he stood about 6'2 or 6'3, He was of a light skinned complexion, and wore a full beard that connected to a mini-sized afro, which he always kept cut and groomed neatly. You could tell by his body structure that he worked out. Bow Bow was a long distance trucked driver who had saved up a little money, married Jackie and bought the 2 story house that they now reside in. Bow Bow quit driving long distance and started driving only Florida routes, so that he wouldn't be gone for long periods of time. All and all he loved his family, they've been together going on 2 years now, and in that period of time he looked at Caddice as his very own "daughter" who he sought to protect.)

Bow Bow continued,

"So, who's the lucky man that was able to keep you from coming home, and not going to school today?"

Candy laughed

"Bow Bow, don't do me like that!"

"I can't wait til you Mama get here"..."because ya'll down like that!"..."You'll tell her, and she'll eventually tell me after during the interrogation."

Caddy went to the refrigerator and grabbed a soda while laughing then turned and asked Bow Bow,

"Where she at?... Anyway?"

"They called her in to work this morning, that's why I'm up, those damn folks at the nursing home trying to take my Mondays you know this suppose to be our lay play day!"..." Anyway, she just not long called to see have you made it in, I think you should call her, for I get the name of this Mystery Man."

Caddy smiled and went up to her room.

As she got in the room she looked through her dresser drawers to find something sexy to wear for Bleak. After searching a few minutes she decided that she would stop by Waymart and grab some cute lil panties. Then she walked to the closet, and got 2 sets of clothes by that time she heard a knock at her room door. She then said,

"You may enter!"

The room door then opened and there Bow Bow stood with a cup of coffee in his hand,

"O Dam, you about to cut out again huh?" When I'ma meet this man?"

"You'll meet him soon enough."

Then Bow Bow continued.

"You know that lil boy, that got killed yesterday, he stayed in the projects where you grew up, I was just reading about it in the paper, girl I'm glad we moved out of there, them damn drugs started taking over and it's a shame how its killing our young people"..."The shit crazy!"

Caddy replied,

"Yah, I knew em, I went to school with him and that was Tasha's boyfriend!"

"O yah," he replied, and then continued, "Tasha seems like a good girl, why would she get herself involved with them type of people. I mean she could've been in the car when that occurred."

Caddy cut him off.

"Bow Bow what you mean? Them type of people?"

Bow Bow replied,

“I’m referring to the life style and what comes with it, death or prison, do you want a man that lives with those consequences each and every day”... “He could be in prison today or dead tomorrow. Now that’s something to think about, look at Tasha this might affect her for years and years to come. Anyways, I’ll let you finish getting ready, but tell Tasha I said I’m sorry about what happened and I’m here for her”...” and as for you Ms. Thing, think about what I said!”

Then he smiled as he closed the bedroom door back.

Caddy replied

“I will!”

As she continued to grab a few outfits placing them in 1 of many shopping bag that hung from her door knob. Candy then headed back down the stairs. She quickly gave Bow Bow a hug and kiss on his cheek as she headed out the door “Love you, I’ll see you later.”

Bow Bow yelled back,

“Call me or your Mama,” Caddy hit the horn as she backed out.

****

Lulu was outside of the hospital, her eyes were swollen from crying. She looked up into the sky while saying in her mind, “God, what do I do now?” After a brief moment she looked around in both direction then she began walking home, which was only 6 or 7 blocks away. As she walked, her mind was racing, trying to consume what she was just told an hour ago. Then she began to think about Beankie, what would he say? And Bleak – How would he react knowing his Mother’s time on earth was limited? How should she tell them? She was confused, hurt and upset, all at the same time.

As she got a block away from Morris Court, she dug in her purse and grabbed her makeup kit that contained a small mirror inside. She looked at her face to see was everything still in place and looked all normal except the swelling around her eyes. She closed the kit and placed it back in her purse and continued walking. As she got closer, she saw people standing in front of the corner store hustling and clowning around as usual. They turned to see her approaching and everybody spoke,

"Hey, Ms. Lulu." "How you doing," She nodded and continued stepping.

When she reached her apartment, she looked at her and Bleaks' Chevys parked side by side. To her they looked beautiful sitting together, almost like a couple that was in love with each other.

She stuck her key in the door and entered her apartment and proceeded to her room, and sat on the bed.

After about 30 minutes or so she got up, grabbed her keys and headed back out the door.

As Caddy reached Wal-Mart, she drove up front to find a place to park close to the entrance, which she was lucky because a car was attempting to back out. As she parked in the spot, she got out and waved at the vehicle while saying, "Thank you," as it left.

As she walked inside, she continued thinking to herself about what Bow Bow was saying and she figured he had a point, and then she began thinking about Bleak as she strolled through the woman's lingerie department. She wondered what life would be like with Bleak. She had a crush on him since high school from the 9th grade, ad that crush was still going. Now that she finally got him she planned on keeping him. She glanced through racks of lingerie, but saw nothing that really caught her eye. Then she went to another rack and there it was she saw a cute lil black lace 2 piece, that appeared to be see through. She grabbed it along with a red one that was made in the same style, but different material. She carried them to the checkout counter, paid the cashier and headed back out to her car.

As she turned the car on and backed out, she put her Keith Sweat CD in the CD player and hit the button to locate her favorite song "Make it last forever." As Keith Sweat sang to her, she started back thinking about Bleak, as she rode down the highway, she asked herself, "I wonder how he felt last night," cause to her it was the best feeling she's had so far in her life. She only had sex twice in her eighteen years of growing up, but she's had orgasms 100's of times, because she often played with herself to ease the tension. She didn't want a boyfriend or a man at the time because she was busy focusing on school, trying to build a career for herself, while she was still young. (It was only when Tasha, her best friend called her telling her that something must have happened to Lulu cause she saw her being carried away in an ambulance. That's when Bleak popped back into her mind, because she knew that Lulu was Bleaks' world and all he had. So she couldn't bear to see or think about Bleak being hurt that's when she realized that she still had those feelings for him. All along she felt like she was missing something and that something, was a someone, named Bleak)

Her spot began to get moist, as she rethought the events that took place last night and how much alive he made her feel. She then said in a whisper, "I need to get my man something to eat," so she stopped at KFC drive thru and ordered a 10 piece box of chicken, a big container of red beans and rice, 2 corns on the cob and 4 biscuits. Then headed to the Residence Inn.

Lulu parked and walked inside Escambia County Health Department. She looked around and saw people everywhere, then said to herself,

"I can't be the only one fucked up."

She then pulled the map Dr. Fazora gave her, from out of her purse and proceed to walked through the crowded clinic. As she saw her destination she noticed a long line of people, then suddenly she spotted someone she knew.

Lulu couldn't believe her eyes nor did she know what to think, so she turned around quickly and saw the sign that read RESTROOM and moved quickly in that direction and entered. When she got to the door, she then immediately went in a stall, locked the door and sat on the toilet. Lulu said in a low tone to herself,

"I can't believe that Nigga up here!"

That someone was "Charlos" or what was left of him anyway. She thought for a minute then continued talking to herself, as if answering herself at the same time, "That Sissy Ass Nigga!... Done gave me this Shit!"

She couldn't help but to start crying all over again.

After, almost an hour passed, she finally got up and come out of the stall. She walked to the mirror to get herself back together, then she peeped out of the bathroom door and headed back past the desk. She was supposed to report to. As she passed by, she saw that the line was now short, she thought about going to get her prescription until she saw another lady behind the desk at a computer who halla'd ,

"Luceal Perkins, Hold on Girl!"

The lady then came from behind the desk to where Lulu stood and embraced her with a hug, then lady then released Lulu

"Girl you don't remember me?"

Lulu replied, "I thought you looked familiar."

(But she really had no idea who the lady was) The lady then continued,

“I’m Dorris Miller, we used to go to school together!”…”Girl you still look good.” “Anyway”…”How you doing?”

“I’m Fine”…” I just dropped somebody off, and I had to use the restroom so I came in!”

“Well, It’s nice to see you, I barely see any of my old classmates, but alright girl, you take care!”

And then the lady began to walk off, but Lulu called her back,

“Hey… Dorris!”

Dorris turned around and walked back to her while saying,

“Yah what’s up girl?”

Lulu continued,

“I just Carlos Johnson in here, he went to school with us for a minute too.”

Dorris replied with a whisper,

“Yah girl, that was a fine man!… But he gone to Waist, Now!”

“What you mean?”

Dorris answered talking even lower than before,

“Girl, he got AIDS, he been coming here to pick up his medication going on 4 years now, and ain’t no telling how long he been infected. Girl,… like I always say… you better ware a rubber… if you want to avoid trouble.”….” and I aint talking about just 1…Girl, I make a Nigga use 3 … some of em more “…” depending on the size.”

She winked and laughed at Lu Lu as she continued,

"Well Girl let me get back to work, if you ever around this way again, stop and halla at me!"

"Alright Dorris" ..."Girl You know I will!"... "But until the next time" ... "It was nice seeing you again!"

CHAPTER 4

Lt. Danny Bernard and Sgt. Mike Matthews were riding around the west side of town in a sky blue 1990 Delta 88 Oldsmobile with dark tinted windows and a pair of Hammers with Vogue tires (which was a car some officers confiscated a few years ago from some people passing through with a few pounds of weed that were from Mobile, Alabama).

They were traveling west on Cervantees until they reached I street and made a right. Danny began speaking as he made the turn,

"Mike, I know you are not familiar with this side of town, so let me fill you in, these projects to your right are "Attucks Court!"

Sgt. Matthews interrupted,

"Danny, I know these projects Pensacola ain't but so big, I just was mainly focused on the eastside of town before I worked my way west."

"I feel you – Clean up one section at a time."

Sgt. Matthews agreed,

"Yep, pretty much."

Then Danny continued, as he made another right turn entering the large apartment complex.

"Yah, Mike, I remember the days ...That, that apartment right there (he pointed as he talked) was where I got my first bust. It use to be a man stayed there, he was a lil older than me, but anyhow he sold heroin...he stayed there with a girl, which it was her apartment. But anyway, she was a nice girl that was until she got on drugs. And Mike, the day I kicked that door down, he was standing in the kitchen with a needle, getting ready to shoot that poison in her arm while her child was on the floor in the kitchen playing. You know of course I beat his ass and I found 2 ounces of uncut heroin!"

"I arrested them both but really tried to get her some help, because I know that low life Muthafucka got her on it and he didn't use."..." but what really fucked me up"..." that coward, blamed it all on her... and the Prosecutor went right along with it.. Plus the girl admitted to it, save that low life... and with the apartment being in her name... He...That coward Muthafucka... got off Scott free!"..." So then he stopped selling heroin and moved to cocaine, I busted his ass again with a ounce and a half of cocaine. But instead of taking him to jail, I put him to work. I called him a bitch, a coward, a Nigger and everything else under the sun...and slapped his punk ass around, every chance I got... He was terrified of me... and Matt...to make this it even sweater.... He was even the one who made the deal with Beankie for us to buy 3 ½ kilos of cocaine, in which your father got killed in the process... but away ....now you know who I'm looking for!"

Danny smirked as his last 2 words side out.

"MY BITCH!"

Sgt. Matthews sat quietly, looking at the cars with rims and flashy colorful paint jobs and the kids running around. He thought to himself (they can't help but to become a product of their environment when they grow up as well, surrounded with these living conditions – low income housing so their Mamas and Daddy's, if available, can't afford to get them spent on cars and clothes and jewelry produced from a sell of one lil rock, you can't help to roll with it)"

Danny looked over at Sgt. Matthews and asked,

"Son is you alright? You haven't said a word since we have been riding through here."

"Yah, I was just putting myself in a drug dealers shoes!""Anyway, I heard you, so does this bitch, have a name??"

Danny replied with a laugh,

"Yeah"... "Arthur Lucas, aka Luke, it's been about 16 years since I saw old Luke... As a matter of fact, I don't even know if he's still living, or still around...but anyhow, I'm finta take you up through the Old Morris Court.. The Hill "was what they called it my days."...." But take note that both of these projects are 1....meaning you fuck with 1...THEY both at your ass!"

As they drove out of Attacks Court, which is about a 4 block radius, they headed up towards Morris Court which is 4 blocks north of Attacks Court.

As they approached Morris Court from a block away Danny proceeded talking,

"Boy, it done changed a lot around here over the years. You see the playground right there; ...it used to be a little building in that field, where the junkies shot up at"..."I guess they done tore it down over the years."

(As they continued riding slowly they reached the entrance of Morris Court, and a car was coming in the opposite direction, so Danny stopped and let it turn in first. Then he hit Sgt. Matthews's shoulder)

"Look a there, that's old school ...Got Dam'it ,as a matter of Fuckin fact!"...That's Benjamin Staples girl's car!"

Sgt. Matthews looked as the champagne pink Chevy turned in the projects.

As Danny continued,

"Damn son, she kept that car up all these years."

Sgt. Matthews then asked, "That is Brad's Mother Right?"

"Yeah Sir...You can bet Your Ass"..."That's Brads Mother!"

They turned in a minute or 2 behind it, and drove around the circle. Morris Court was a small 1 way in, 1 way out apartment complex with a road that went around like a circle. They spotted where Lulu had parked and saw another Chevy next to it.

Danny responded with excitement,

"DAMM!"..."That must be her sons shit!"..."but that's kind of old school for a young boy considering the rims!...Dam Son!.. Look at that 2 Chevys, yellow and pink, with rag tops, Cragar Rims on Vogues!"...I know you don't know anything about that"...cuz, you use to seeing the Dayton's, vinyl tops, and Candy paint...Thing going on right now!...But that Right There!" ..." Is from my ERA!" ..."Shit, that's how the Playa's Rolled."

They drove on past and headed out of Morris Court as they got back on J Street (which is the road you turn off to enter Morris Court) they turned left and came to a stop sign. Danny then started back talking,

"Now that store there across the street, that's where the dope is regularly sold at around here, it's been that way for years, it used to be a club next to it, but I closed that Muthafucka years ago."

Danny then made another left while still talking,

"This here on your right is all considered Morris Court to me!"

Sgt. Matthews looked to see another section of the project buildings that continued on down the street.

"Damn Danny, they got a little interesting set up all around here...We done drove through 3 apartment complexes"..." but I don't see much activity!"

Danny laughed...

"Son!"... "You really don't you know shit, Huh?"..." Look and listen!"..." the streets is like the Military"...."when a high ranked official... out of your Squadron dies!"..." the whole platoon mourns!"..."They mourning, Son"..."They mourning!"

Candy placed the hotel key card in the door, as she grabbed the door knob and pushed the door open, and then she yelled,

"Honey, I'm home."

Bleak then appeared in his boxers from out of the bedroom,

"Where you been?" he asked, while walking to meet her.

She said, as she sat the KFC bag on the kitchen counter,

"I took your Mama to her Doctor's appointment, I stopped by my house, I stopped by Wal-Mart and I stopped to get you something to eat!"…"Why you miss me?"

By that time Bleak had his arms around her standing face to face as she told him, her whereabouts. Bleak then replied while looking into her eyes,

"Yah, I miss you." Then he let go

"Now what you got in that bag, because I'm hungry."

She patted his stomach while replying.

"Baby just chill, I'ma feed you!"

She headed into the bedroom with the Wal-Mart bag in her hand. Bleak went looking in the KFC bag, until she yelled from the bedroom,

"Sit down Baby and let me feed you."

Shortly after she came out of the bedroom then Bleak stood up and stared because she returned in the black 2 piece lace lingerie set. Bleak couldn't help but to give her a head to toe evaluation.

Candy was beautiful and sexy, she stood 5'3 with pretty pecan brown skin and long natural silky black hair that hung shoulder length. At that moment he really saw what D-Boy was talking about. Candy had a set of small, but healthy breasts with chocolate colored nipples that he could see through the silky looking bra she had on. Plus, he couldn't forget the lil fat round ass she had, cause that was the last position he had her in before falling asleep last night. Candy also had a pretty lil chubby toes, with powder blue nail polish, that matched her finger nails. Candy was all natural and the belly ring she wore, had a gold heart with small diamonds around it and it hung from her navel, which made her body look even more beautiful. Candy was somebody worth having, somebody you would introduce to the world, before taking her home to Mama.

Candy stood there modeling for him, then suddenly she said,

"Nigga, Say something!"

Bleak then snapped back into reality and replied,

"Baby you look good! Just tell me what it is you trying to do?"

She smile, "Boy you late....It's already done." Then she walked into the kitchen and started preparing him a plate.

Here you Baby"... "Eat up, I'm finta go in here and call Tasha to see how she doing!"

"Alright!"

Bleak replied through a mouth stuffed with chicken.

Candy went in the room and called Tasha, when the phone rang Tasha picked up on the first one,

"Hello,"

Tasha answered in a low tone.

"You alright Girl?"

Tasha then began talking when she realized it was her best friend,

"Yah, alright girl, I'm still trying to think, that this is all just a bad dream. Girl, I'm pregnant and my baby daddy died, my Mama don't know and you're the only one

I told and Ms. Anna Bell just figured I was. Girl I don't know what to think or do. I done cried so much, and so hard until I can't cry no more, I just been laying in the bed since yesterday, but anyway I'm glad you called and by the way, where you at cause your Mama called!"

"I been with Bleak."

Then Tasha continued talking,

"Finally you done got what you wanted, huh?"

"Yep," Candy replied.

"Well I'm happy for ya'll. How is he taking everything?"

"He still fucked up about it, I just keep trying to take his mind off it, at least until the funeral, because I know him and Crash, they gone try to do something."

Tasha interrupted saying, "Girl at first I was feeling like something should be done, but now I don't think I can stand it cause what if one of them get killed also, this should be a lesson if anything, for they can stop doing what they doing. Cause all it brings is Death or Prison!"

"Girl you been talking to Bow Bow?"

"Yep, and I feel like he right, well anyways, Girl I'm alright, I just want to be alone until Saturday!"

"Alright call me if you need to talk, I'm at the Residence Inn Room 224, the number is 433-2107."

They both exchanged Byes and hung up the phone.

CHAPTER 5

Crash didn't feel like hustling or doing anything else until after D-Boy's funeral. He sat at the kitchen table along with Buggaloo and Tig loading up the guns that they just not long ago purchased. Suddenly Crash stood up,

"Man I'm finta ride, I need to clear my mind cuz ya'll sitting around here like this a normal day or something!"... "Nigga...A Nigga just killed my Dog!"

Tig interrupted

"Nigga he our Homie too, what you think we don't give a damn or something? I just figure it like this...let's get rid of all this shit and bury our homie first...then kill the killer and afterwards, we go rent us a place...a new trap, with the same set up!"...Now, Do that makes sense to You?"

After a pause Crash replied,

"That's why you and Bleak the brains. I can understand that, but I ain't up to it, so you'll proceed with everything, I just need some time to think before I go crazy."

"Do what you need, Homie, Me and Buggaloo got this!"..." Just don't go do nothing stupid, you hear me!" Crash said as he walked to the door,

"I got you Boss."

After he walked out slamming the door behind him, Buggaloo went to peep out the window watching Crash as he burned rubber out of the parking lot. Then Buggaloo turned back in Tig's direction to see him still placing bullets into the clips that were scattered along the table. Buggaloo then shook his head

"Boy, I ain't no fool by a long shot, something tells me that you already know who shot D-Boy."

Tig stopped what he was doing and looked at Buggaloo for a minute then replied,

"I knew an hour after it happened but why tell him or Bleak!"... "I'm trying to do this shit and get away with it. Now Crash on the other hand, he'll have a point to prove and he'll want Niggas to know and end up with a life sentence and as for Bleak, he madder than a Muthafucka. He was there when it happened so he would automatically go against his better judgment. So I'ma let em both cool off."

Buggaloo then shook his head in agreement,

"Boy you got Cartel Potential, I like that, you kind of remind me of me once upon a time. Nigga Fuck Tig, I'ma call you Loo-Tig-Arotchie."

Tig smiled as he continued placing the bullets into the clips with a towel over his hand to avoid fingerprints on the shell casings. After an hour and a half past Tig looked at Buggaloo,

"Grab 2 of them cookies, so we can cut em up, it's time to open up shop."

****

(Knock, Knock)

"Who is it?"

"Hey, Ms. Lulu," a small voice replied then continued, "Ms. Anna Bell wants you!"

As Lulu opened the door she saw a lil girl running off down the sidewalk. Lulu then turned around and walked in her room and put on her house shoes. Then she went out the door and walked down the sidewalk to Ms. Anna Bell's apartment.

Ms. Anna Bell was seated on the front porch as Lulu approached.

"Hey Lulu...what girl, you gone sit in the house all day?"

"After all that's been going on Ms. Anna Bell, I just sit in there and drown myself in misery!"..."But anyhow Ms. Anna Bell, How are you doing?"

Ms. Anna Bell nodded.

As Lulu sat down on the porch

Ms. Anna Bell began talking,

"Honey… you alright? You don't look too well. What did the Doctor say?"

Lulu didn't respond, instead she began to cry, then Ms. Anna Bell said,

"Honey everything gone be alright, just pray about it, like I do."

Ms. Anna Bell figured Lulu had gotten some disturbing news, but just played it off and continued talking,

"Yep, everything gone be alright Daryl's in a better place!"

Then after a minute or two Ms. Anna Bell said,

"Well Baby, I just sent that lil girl down there to get you out the house for a second, but I can see you still need some time alone, so I'ma just sit out here to calm my nerves."

Lulu then stood up

"Yah, Ms. Anna Bell it was nice of you to get me out, but I'ma need a lil more time to myself!"

"Take all the time you need Baby."

As Lulu walked off she stopped and turned back around and asked,

"Hey Ms. Anna Bell where's Sue Ann I haven't seen her since D-Boy," (she stopped).

Ms. Anna Bell replied,

"O Baby she been locked up in her room, she'll come out to eat but that's it. She just aint' ready to face anybody yet, and the good thang about it, (she broke down in a whisper) I feel she trying to stop smoking that crack…You know God works in mysterious ways, even thou the Devil is in us all."

Then Lulu turned and walked off with a smile.

Crash pulled up in the liquor store parking lot on the corner of "N" Street and Cervantes. He looked around to see if there was anybody he knew standing outside, then suddenly he saw his cousin "JJ" approaching his car.

"Crash, what's going on, you alright?"

"Yah, man I just need you grab me a 5th of Hennessy and some cups of ice,"

"I got you cuzzin, it's on me. I know your boy gone and you need something to mellow your mind. Just park, I'll be back in a second."

Crash pulled in a space between two cars as he watched JJ run in the liquor store.

JJ was Crash's first cousin, his Daddy's brother son, they barely saw each other but every time they did, it was love. JJ liked selling Coke and snorting it also, so he basically hustled to get high, but he stayed sharp and kept money in his pocket. On top of that JJ was cooler than a Muthafucka plus he wasn't anybody to be to fuck with, if it came down to some gangsta shit.

JJ was 7 years older than Crash, and once upon a time, he was the man , that's before he went to prison. Now he just hustled to get by and get high. Nothing more nothing less.

As JJ returned he jumped in the passenger's side,

"Let's ride lil cousin, for I can make sure you don't do nothing out of the ordinary. Plus you need somebody to collaborate with, you know what I say – Blood thicker than water, but mud thicker than both and D-Boy...he was your dirty."

Crash pulled out of the parking lot while JJ fixed him and his drinks, then he pulled out a sack of weed and grabbed a blunt out of the bag the 5th of Hennessy was in. JJ rolled the blunt and fired it up, then leaned back into the seat, while at the same time grabbing Crash's CD case and strolling through it. Crash was sipping on the cup of Hennessy as he drove in deep thought. JJ suddenly said,

"I found something right here to set off the moment." Then put a CD in the CD player and pushed the button to the track he wanted his lil cousin to listen to,

"I never seen a Man cry, until I seen a Man die" by Scarface.

Crash felt that and turned it up even louder.

****

(Ring, Ring....Ring, Ring)

"Hello,"

Candy replied in a sleepy drained out voice. Then she heard her Mother's voice,

"Girl, you wasn't gone call me, I had to call Tasha to find out where my daughter at?"

"O Mama, I'm sorry,"

"Where... Bleak at?"

"He's sleep," Candy whispered.

"What ya'll Doing?.., At the Residence Inn?"

"We just chillin Mama."

"CHILLIN MY ASS!"... "Ya'll doing more than just chillin. I can hear that in your voice."

"Mama, stop it!"

"How long ya'll staying there?"

"I think he got it for the whole week or at least up until D-Boy's funeral."

"I'm sorry to hear about that boy dying the way that he did. Tasha trying to hold it all in but she gone eventually break. I can hear it in her voice."

"Mama what you is a voice analyzer?"

"No...but I can read lil girls, because I was a lil girl myself. But anyway, ya'll balling out ain't it?"..." I know you been looking at that boy for a long time. All I can say is girl... you just like yo Mama, we gets our man. You know Bow Bow trying to figure out... who "THE MYSTERY MAN, is? But your secret safe with me, that's why I waited so late to call!"

Candy looked at the clock on the TV and saw that it was 1:45AM

"What you doing up this late at night?"

"I been waiting, for Bow Bow to fall asleep, for I can call you ..."O yah, also you know Janay and Kim called me.... they say, they were coming home to go to Darl's funeral"..." You know their doing well up there in California...at least that's what they say. But anyway, I'ma let your lil wore out ass go back to sleep. I hope you don't miss school in the morning, like you did today!"

"I'm going Mama,"... "And by the way, it's a new day right now!"

"Girl you know what I mean."

Jackie and Candy then both exchanged Byes and hung up the phone.

Afterwards, Candy looked over at Bleak, to see him sound asleep. Then she went to thinking about Janay and Kim. They both had got accepted to UCLA on basketball scholarships. They all grew up together in the projects and attended the same school. But Candy had carried a lil bit of jealousy in her heart for Janay. She didn't look better than Candy nor was she finer than Candy. Candy just knew what Janay, thought nobody knew....that her and Bleak were fucking on the DL. They both had managed to play it off good, they fooled everybody except her. She even saw Bleak climb through Janay's bedroom window one night. Candy was so mad, that she wanted to sneak out the house and throw a brick through Janay's bedroom window so the glass could fall on the both of them and hopefully they got caught in the process by Janay's parents.

Candy knew that the thought was childish, and beside Bleak wasn't her man.

"But times has changed and shit is different now,"

She said in a whisper to herself, then continued on with the thought of Janay coming back in town, while asking herself,

"What if this bitch... tries to fuck my man!"... "Or what if he tries to fuck her?"

So before she knew it, she punched Bleak in the chest.

Bleak awoke instantly, "What the hell?"

Then he looked over at Candy to see her sitting up in the bed.

"Baby?"..." You just hit me or something?"

"Bleak we need to talk!"

"Yah... I guess so...with you hitting on me and shit."

Candy continued,

"First off, where we stand?"

"Where we lying?"

"What kind of answer is that?"..." I asked you where we stand."

"Yah, and I answered you with where we lying!"..." We're in this bed together, right?"

She smirked while saying,

"Yea, we are!"..." but my Mama just told me... that Kim and Janay were coming home for D-Boy's funeral!"

"That's good"..."so why you mad?"

"I'm mad, because I know about you and Janay ASS!"

Bleak immediately cut her off:

"Look here Baby, I don't know what it is... you think you know, but whatever it is, you need to leave it buried!"..."Because!"..." you go digging up shit!"..."the dirt isn't gone fit back in that hole... exactly how it came out."

Candy didn't know what the hell Bleak meant, but it did make her feel good to get it get off her chest. The more she thought about it his response. She realized he was simply saying,

"Let the past, be the past."

Bleak laid back and pulled the covers back over his chest. Candy then leaned over and kissed him.

"Okay"..." Baby you can go back to sleep"..."But don't make me have to dig in your chest about Janay!" Then she got back under the covers and laid her head on his shoulder.

As Bleak, closed his eyes he couldn't help but to begin reminiscing about Janay.

Janay was 5'11 when he last seen her, before she went to UCLA. As he remembered: Janay was pretty as hell; she was a red bone, with long curly hair that had an auburn color tone to it. She had hazel brown eyes and a nice petite, slender trim shape.

But what Bleak enjoyed most, was that Janay was an undercover freak. She learned how to fuck from sneaking around in her mother's room watching her porno VHS collection, plus ...Janay, was the first girl that Bleak had sex with and to him, that's all it was "Sex".

Bleak always liked Candy, and now with them being together as a couple, he felt ...Dedicated! Similar to how his father felt about Lu Lu, but he did wonder how Candy knew, and by her knowing, "Who else knew?"

After a few minutes or so he slowly drifted back off to sleep.

****

Crash and JJ was sitting in the Box Chevy outside of the R.K.'s Club & Bar as people began coming out, and for some reason the club looked thicker than it usually be on what everybody called "Monday Night Raw". As they sat observing the crowd of people especially females, Crash began reminiscing about the first 3 nights him and D-Boy made their grand appearances. They had just got their cars out of the paint shop and couldn't wait until night fall, for they could represent "Pressure World" to the fullest. Crash even got D-Boy to dress out of his normal style. The first night, which was a Saturday night they went to the "Player's Club". Both of them were Polo Down (Casual) and each wore the same color of the car they drove. They clowned that night, tossed stacks of 20's in the air and watched how the girls were going crazy, fighting over the money and all, and watching the jealousy that arose in Nigga's eyes as they took over the picture area. Then D-Boy ended up buying the camera from the picture man, to take pictures with the 4 girls they took to the Hilton Hotel to have a "Freak Fiesta".

The next 2 night was an instant replay that ended at R.K's, which was the last night he had been there.

Crash started laughing to himself, and then came back to reality when he saw a girl standing at his window. He looked to his right side, as he pushed the button for the window to come down and noticed that JJ was gone, then he turned his head back to the girl.

"What's Happening Lil Mama?"

"O hey"..."I been seeing, this car around, a few times ...and wanted to take a look at the driver!"

"O yah,"

Crash responded and continued,

"O Okay...So now, what's your next move?"

"I really don't know, but I'ma start by giving you my number,"

As she rummaged through her purse, looking for a pen Crash gave her a quick look over. He first saw that she was thick as hell; she had on a tight lil snake skin looking mini skirt that gripped around her ass perfectly exposing its full potential. She was dark and pretty and had about 2 or 3 gold teeth as he could see. "O, I'm sorry, it took me a second, I just got so much shit in my purse it's hard to find anything." As she passed him her number she said,

"I saw you checking me out too!"..."You like what you see?"

"Shit, the jury still out on that!"..."Cuz I really couldn't see that much!"

"Well I'ma back up a lil and spin around for you"...that way, you won't have to get out the car!"

As she did that, Crash shook his head while saying to himself,

"Yah"... "This Black Muthafucka, Bad!" Then she came back closer to the window.

"Now is that good enough for you?"

"Yep!"

But before he could say anything else, he saw a dude come up from behind her and grabbed her by her hair saying,

"Bitch you trying me, huh?"

As he begun dragging her away, while yelling over to another dude who was approaching him,

"Man, I just caught this Bitch over there at that PUSSY ASS NIGGA CAR!"

Crash heard that and opened the door and stood up between it facing the direction the dude was dragging the in girl.

He then heard someone tap the hood of his car, so he slightly turned his head around and saw that it was JJ.

"Kin Folks, What's Happenin?" JJ halla'd

Crash replied in a loud tone (as he turned his head back around)

"I'm TRYING TO FIGURE OUT WHO THIS FUCK NIGGA TALKING ABOUT!"

The guy immediately let the girl hair go, and walked back towards Crash. But as soon as he got close enough, Crash came from in between the door with a half empty bottle of Hennessey, cuffed in his hand.

He quickly grabbed the guy by his chain, and began beating him in the head with the bottle.

JJ halla'd out loudly.

"Beat that Nigga Ass Folks!... and AIN'T NOBODY GONE DO SHIT ABOUT IT!"

After Crash continuously kept hitting him in the head and face with the bottle, the dude fell to the ground bleeding heavily, Crash then began kicking him.

He suddenly stopped when he realized how fucked up the dude was, he then kneeled down and whispered in his ear

"Nigga, tell your Girl bye ...cause she going with me!"

As he stood back up he looked over in her direction

"You Coming?"

And unbelievably she complied.

JJ halla'd out while laughing as he was getting in the back seat

"Yeah, That's how we do it! ...Beat a Nigga Ass...and Take His Old Lady!"

As Crash speeded out of the parking lot, JJ went to talking,

"Look here lil Mama, that Nigga gone kill you" ..."Naw, Fuck that!"..."Cuzo.. That Nigga gon kill, the both of ya'll!"

JJ was laughing and clowning all the way home, and when Crash stopped to drop him off, JJ asked

"Cuzo, can I halla at you for a minute?"

Crash got out and they walked to the back of the car.

"Man, what the hell you doing?"..."Folks, I don't like this shit, but I'm down with you to the fullest, but Nigga I wouldn't have that bitch in my car!" Crash looked at JJ eye to eye,

"I got this Kin-Folks," and got back in the car.

As Crash then drove off he asked the girl,

"What's your name?"

"Porsha."

He then continued

“So Ms.Porsha?”… “What the hell, you thinking about?”…”trying to halla at a NIgga… at the club …and your man there too?”

“That ain’t my man!”…” I was fucking with him for a minute, plus trying to help him come up, but all he was doing was bringing me down!”

“O Yah… so you a hustler, Ha ?”

“Yah, I try to do a lil something”… “I got a Shorty to take care of, and I don’t need NO Nigga for shit!”

“O Okay I feel you!”…”So, Where you stay?”

“I stay in Sunrise Apartments!“

“O Okay!” …”Well I’m finta take you there!”… “And Lil Mama I wish you luck with that Nigga!”…”the only reason I got involved… was because of the statement he made…but as I see it.. I just met you 30 minutes ago and already put myself in some trouble… and TROUBLE!”…” I don’t really need right now!”

As he pulled into Sunrise Apartments, she told him to stop and as she got out, she turned around

“Well Crash Thank You!” I appreciate the ride…and hopefully we get a chance to link up!” …”Shit, you know 2 devoted minds, can build an empire!”…You need to think about that!”

Crash replied,

“Okay!”…”I’ll Halla!”

And he pulled off, without even giving her a chance to close the door.

CHAPTER 5

"Bleak, wake up Baby,"

Candy said as she shook Bleak awoke.

"What time is it?"

"Baby, its 7:30 and I'm finta go to school, I wanted to know if you needed my car?"

"Nah, I'm straight Baby,"

Bleak replied, and then continued,

"I'll call Tig or Crash to come get me if I decide to go somewhere. But anyway what time you get out?"

"I'll be out about 1 or no later than 2!"

"Alright!"

He replied as he began to cover his face with the sheets that covered the rest of his body.

"Alright?"..."Dam, I don't get a kiss or nothing before I go?"

Candy exclaimed as she was fixing her hair in the mirror, while looking back at him through the mirror.

"Yeah!" Bleak replied, then continued,

"But I know!"…"you ain't gone make me get up... to give it to you."

Candy then walked from the dresser back over to the bed, where he laid and kissed him.

"Bye Baby,"…."See you later!"

Bleak laid there for a minute until he realized that he couldn't fall back to sleep. He then picked up the phone and called home...After 3 rings Lulu picked up,

"Hello."

"Mama, what's up?"

"Nothing much, Baby,"

"What happened at the hospital?"

Lulu froze before saying,

"I'll tell you later, Baby."

"Everything Alright?...Ain't it?"

Lulu replied again,

"I'll tell you later!"…" Anyway, since you've been lying up with Candy, I ain't heard from you, and that's not normal." (She began laughing) "Shit, it got to be good, to keep you away from Mama!"

"Mama"…"You Crazy!"

"Mama ain't Crazy...I see my lil man in love!"…"and I'm happy you finally found yourself a girlfriend!"

Bleak smiled at that statement.

"Mama come and get me!"..."for we can go to breakfast or something!" He then told her where he was at and they hung up the phone.

****

When Lulu pulled into the Hotel parking lot, she saw Bleak coming out the lobby, approaching the car. As he got in he gave her a hug and kissed her on the cheek. Lulu asked,

"So, Where to Baby?"

"Where ever you go Mama... is alright with me, I'm just hungry."

Lulu halla'd out,

"IHOP," as she pulled off.

****

When they arrived at IHOP, Lulu saw that it was crowded so they went up the highway to Waffle House.

As they went in, Lu Lu chose a table next to the window overlooking the highway's early morning traffic.

When the waitress arrived Lulu ordered a steak and egg special and a large orange juice. Bleak got a ham and cheese omelet with bacon and grits and a large sweet tea.

As they waited on their food, Lulu began talking,

"Baby, you know your birthday next month which is a few weeks, you'll be 18 then so what you gone do?"

"Mama, I don't know, I had forgotten until the other day. I went and paid for the hotel, I handed the lady behind the desk my ID like I was 18 already, but she let me slide and gave me the room anyway. But Mama with all that's been going on, I look at birthdays like any other day."

"Baby, I haven't had a chance to talk to you about what happened, that day with you and Daryl, plus I knew you weren't ready to talk about it anyway, but now that you had time. Baby, what happened?"

"We were just riding and a car hit us from behind, then when D-Boy got out they went to shooting. I pulled off and turned around to get D-Boy.... (He paused; as water began forming in the corners of his eyes).

Lulu placed her hand over his hand,

"Baby don't worry about it. I get the picture."

Then after a brief moment she continued,

"Baby, you should look at this... along with everything else, that's going on. Baby life is too short and with the route you going...makes it even shorter....I pray, I live long enough to see you get yourself together, because Mama ain't gone be around forever..So you need to be working on that as soon as possible!"

Bleak smirked

"Mama, you talking like you an old lady, or you about to die are something ...You only 37 ....So I got plenty time to change!"

He continued laughing, while wiping the few tears away, and removing his arms from the table, as the waitress preceded to place their plates in front of them.

As Lu Lu began eating, she kept thinking about what her son just said

("Ma you talking like an old lady or you about to die or something!")

. Those words made her question herself

"Dam, how can I tell my son?"..."That I'm already dead!!"... "They just ain't covered the whole yet!!"...

After they finished eating, Lu Lu asked

"Where to now, Baby?",

"Home", Bleak replied, as they walked out and got back in the car.

At the moment Lu Lu felt good, because it's been a long time since her and Bleak spent some real quality time together. They both sat silently as they rode with the windows down, listening to The Isleys –Living for the Love of you!

As they pulled into Morris Ct, Bleak spotted Buggaloo and Tig sitting on the porch. As Lu Lu got closer to pass by, Bleak yelled out the window

"I'll be over in a minute!".

Buggaloo stood up with excitement

"Yes Sir ....Come back and halla at you Boys!!" ..."We Ain't Going Nowhere!"

As Lu Lu parked in front of her apartment, Bleak hopped out with his keys in hand and opened the door to his car, whiling turning around to see Lu Lu exiting hers .Bleak exclaimed with a smile

"Wow, Ma "..."I can't believe, how much I really miss my Baby!"..."I almost, forgot how beautiful she was!"

Lu Lu laughed as she was heading in her apartment

"Boy, you silly!"..."but yeah, She is tight! ...But, you can never compare a soda, TO CHAMPAGNE ...That's Classy Right there!"

Bleak couldn't do nothing but shake his head

"Whatever Ma, You got that!"

****

As Bleak silently sat in the car with the engine running, he began to think about D-Boy all over again, slowly replaying every moment of that day in his mind. As tears slowly ran down his face, he turned the engine off, got out and proceeded to Ms. Anna Bell's apartment.

When he got to the screen door and tapped on it, Ms. Anna Bell halled

"Baby, It's open"..."Wow, I been expecting you!"..."God is good"..."Ain't He?"

Bleak walked in and headed to the kitchen where she was "You Hungry Baby?"

"No mamma..I'm stuffed..me and Lu Lu just left Waffle house"..."But it show-do.. Smell good in here... As always!"

As he took a seat at the table he continued

"Ms. Anna Bell I was thinking, how we go about getting D-Boy ...I mean Daryl's car back? '" ..." For I can at least get it fixed up and place it in storage"..."Crazy as it sounds... that car represents D-Boy, on 4 wheels!".

Ms Anna Bell chuckled

" Yes Lord, It does...and Bleak that's a funny thing you asked about that, because somebody called yesterday and said I can come down to the city impound and get it ....I know them Muthfuckas was trying to be funny...Cuz the whole police station know I ain't got no dam legs".

They both laugh for a moment, then Ms. Anna Bell face turned serious as she whispered

"You thought about what I asked you?"

"Yes, Ma'am...and your wish in my command Ms Anna Bell, I Promise you!!"

Ms. Anna Bell smiled

"I know you will Baby...Just take your time!"..."Now give me a hug and go tend to your business ...Before that darn Buggaloo, come knocking on my dam door!"..

Bleak laughed as he exited the door

"You too Funny, Ms Anna Bell, Love you!"

"Love Too', Baby", she replied.

As Bleak, approached Buggaloo's porch where they were seated.. Buggaloo and Tig immediately stood up to embrace him

"Whats up Homie ? ".

"I'm good! "..." How you'll holding up?"

"We are holding up!"..." Considering, the circumstance!"

Tig responded then continued.

"We got close to 80gs in the pot and 43 circles left on the business side of things...Plus, I got something to show you."

As they entered the apartment Buggaloo went to his room and returned with a duffle bag. Bleak opened it and saw the guns inside then looked back up at Tig

"I Like That!"

"That's what homies are foe...We all do our part ...Now you know when we punish whoever responsible ...We gone need to find us another location, cuz its gone get hot as fish grease around here!"

"Yeah, I know"..." Plus we gone need to find a new source, but all that can wait until after D-Boys funeral...then it's up there!" ..."Anyway you'll Niggas hold the fort down , I'll be at Residence Inn room 224".

Buggaloo went to laughing as he picked up duffle bag to return it to his room. Bleak asked

"Dam Buggaloo, what's so dam funny?

"THE POWER OF PUSSY....You know, that's what got Adam kicked out the garden!"

Bleak laughed.

"Man Fuck You!!"..And Tig you laughing but you need to try.. Getting some!!...

After the laughter came to a minimum Bleak continued

"Man... Where is Crash?"

"Don't worry, He good!...He just blowing off a lil steam...He been in the Red Bricks (Attucks Ct)!"...I got my ears on em!...He Good!"

"O Kay, Well tell em to hit me up!"

Bleak then returned home and sat with Lu Lu for few minutes; afterwards he gave her hug and got in his car, and headed back to the hotel.

Chapter 6

The phone rang 4 times before SGT. Matthews picked up,

“Hello, Hello!”

“Rise and Shine, Son!”

Mike immediately recognized the voice

“Dam Danny, What’s going on?’

“Work as usual Son!”

“Danny, Man it’s my off day”…” Plus I haven’t seen nor heard from you in almost a week!”

“Shit, I been working Son”…”I done recruited me 3 team players!”

“HuH?”…”Danny, It’s to dam early in the morning…So tell me what the hell are talking about?”

“Informants, Son…Informants!”…” Dam, I’m beginning to question how the hell you became a SGT!”…” Anyway Son!.. You are going to learn a lot from me!!”…”And by-the-way …I’m on my way to come get you!”…”So hang up, AND GET READY!”

As Mike climbed out of bed and begun to get dressed, his wife woke up and looked at him

“Honey!”…”Where are you going?”

“To work!”

She then sat up in the bed.

“DAM IT, MIKE!”…”IT’S YOUR FUCKIN DAY OFF!”

“Babe, I want be long”…”I just going with Danny to check something out…And I’ll be right back!”…” I Promise!”

(But actually, he didn’t know where he was going or what he was doing)

She watched as he was putting on his shoes

“Mike FUCK you!”…”I can’t believe this SHIT, and look how it is so easy… for you just walk out of my life!”…”It’s like we done became fucking roommates or something!”…”WE DON’T EVEN FUCK OFTEN, LIKE WE USE TOO…DAM!”

Mike replied with a frown on his face.

“Come On Babe….Don’t start, Please Don’t start!”

His wife name was Sandy Matthews. Sandy was 35 and stood about 5’8’. She had long sandy brown hair and a pretty golden brown tan. Sandy was slim and sexy. She had a little round shaped ass, but her breast was what really brought out her figure.

Sandy worked as a Clerk of Court in the traffic division at the Escambia County Judicial Building.

Sandy loved her husband, and without a doubt she knew he loved her. But she felt second to his job and that was beginning to become a problem.

Mike herd a horn blowing outside.

"Sandy….Honey, I promise I'll be back in a few!"

"Whatever, Mike!"…"BYE!", She replied with a sarcastic tone.

When Mike walked outside, Sandy stood watching from their bedroom window as he climbed in the passenger side of a Sky Blue Delta 88. As the car back out of their driveway and pulled off, Sandy took a deep breath and climbed back in the bed.

As she laid for a minute in deep thought, she suddenly said to herself in a whisper "Fuck him!"

Sandy then slide out of her night grown and begun touching herself. One of the two habits she picked up a lil over 2 months ago. As she continued rubbing the rim of vagina in slow circler motion, she closed her eyes and tried to imagine Mike inside of her.

As she felt herself getting moist, she stopped with a look of frustration upon her face, because she wanted the real thing. After a brief moment, sandy climbed out of bed and reached deep in-between her bed mattress to retrieve her other new found pleasure----A Sock that contained and 8 ball of cocaine.

As Danny and SGT Matthews rode off, SGT Matthews finally asked

"Danny Wsup?"…"You dragged me out the house on my off day!"…"Sandy's pissed!"…"So where the Hell, are we going?"

Danny laughed as he replied.

"TO A FUNERAL, SON!"…."TO- A- MUTHERFUCKING- FUNERAL!"